ELEMENTAL WARS BOOK ONE

NERVOUS WATERS

TRACY KORN

From the Book of Metatron

In the beginning...

1 the Lord saw nothingness, and in it, he placed a seed. From the seed grew the Tree of Life, and from this tree sprang the fruit of the Gnomes, who were of the earth.

2 They were to bring forth the plants and animals that would populate the great landscape, but alas, the Gnomes lacked a vital spirit.

3 The Lord saw this and created the Undines, who were of the water. They were to nourish the earth so life would spring forth, but alas, the Undines, too, lacked a vital spirit.

4 The Lord then created the Sylphs, who were of the air. They were to gather the water into the skies and deliver it unto the earth, but this would not come to pass, for even they lacked a vital spirit.

5 At last, the Lord created the Salamanders, who were of the great fire. The Lord said unto the Salamanders, change the water into air so it will rise high enough to penetrate the earth.

6 The Salamanders obeyed, and life sprang forth. The Lord saw this and said that it was good.

7 The Gnomes, Undines, Sylphs, and the Salamanders had become united as one vital spirit called The Elementals.

8 The world was theirs during the unrecorded time, and for a while, there was peace.

Chapter 1

Three halfling girls swam toward me in the distance, too young to be this close to the boundary, but too old, apparently, to be scared by dragnet and harpoon stories.

They stopped abruptly and clutched something to their chests, each of them darting in a different direction when they saw me. One of them was heading toward the winding southeast reef, which meant she'd have nowhere to go if I could catch the end of her wake.

And of course I could. Halflings were fast, but they weren't agile. She soon found herself cornered in the tall coral, too close to the surface for an Undine under fifteen years old to jump over without the last rays of sunlight turning her skin to stone. At least, that was what we told them. It kept them from attacking the human boats that passed through our waters.

"I'm sorry, Your Highness!" she echoed. "Here, take it!" She extended her arms to me, but I couldn't make out what they held at this distance. Her silver hair started to blacken as it fanned behind her like an explosion of ink. She was even younger than I thought, still bare-chested and yellow-gilled instead of the blue-green of a mature Undine.

"Cora! *There* you are," Reed, another lieutenant in the Queen's Guard, called to me over my shoulder. His silver hair was falling out of its binding, suggesting he'd come through rough waters. He swam to my side, then noticed the halfling. "Oh…what's in your arms, little one?" he asked her sweetly. I forced myself to let this fatherly approach play out only because I promised myself I would rake Reed's scales the second she was out of sight.

"Just tithings from the ship..." she squeaked, extending her arms to us and offering Reed a little smile.

"What ship?" I asked, studying the items in her grasp. A chain of gold and two of silver, one of these attached to a watch. "Who gave you these?"

"The men who fell from the ship near the sandbar, Your Highness—only...they didn't *exactly* give them to me. But they weren't going to use them anymore," she insisted, her yellow eyes widening and darkening like her hair. "Mara told us they were tithings. The humans are in *our* world. It's the least they can do!"

Of course it was Mara, I thought, shaking my head. "Is *that* what she told you? What's your name?"

"Opal, Your Highness."

"You don't need to call me that. Do you understand what happens to Undine who attack ships, Opal? Who disobey the queen's explicit instructions to stay away from humans?"

"But Mara—"

"*Mara* will get you gutted on a ship deck or worse! And that's if you manage to keep from turning to stone first...you're not old enough to be this close to the surface!"

"Yes, Your High—I mean, *Cora.*"

"Do you even know what this is?" I grabbed the chain with the attached silver casing. "The humans call it a *watch.* Do you know why? Because it *watches* everything you do and everywhere you go. That's how they know where to find you."

"Mara didn't say—"

"Go home to your parents, Opal," Reed cooed at her, smoothing her hair, which was pulsing the spectrum of silver to black like a cuttlefish. I took the other trinkets from her, but she didn't even seem to notice as she smiled up at Reed and reached to touch the two swirled lines of his shoulder rank tattoo.

I swatted her hand away and gripped her chin. "Opal, if I see you out past the boundary again, I'll lock you in the hole myself, do you understand?"

She nodded quickly, turning completely black as she sped past me toward the cove like an eel in the night. I rounded on Reed.

He held his hands up, like that would keep me from gutting him. "Hey, hey! A princess shouldn't be violent..."

"Then I guess it's a good thing I'm also a soldier! Did I ask for your help? Because I don't recall echoing for you to *pardon* her."

"Listen, you should be thanking me! I came out here because—wait, *pardon* her? You were actually going to charge her? She's just a halfling, Cora." Reed leveled his green eyes at me and cocked his head to the side. "I mean, come on. You were making her shadow over having some human trash."

"How do you think she'd feel if one of those monsters pulled her up in a dragnet? Do you think cooing at her would save her then?" I swam past him to find Mara, making a point to knock into him.

"Cora, wait!"

"They *need* to fear the boundary waters, Reed!" I echoed back to him without turning around. "We have no power there!"

I gripped the chain trinkets in my hand so tightly, they bit into my skin. The pain propelled me out of the coral field and back to the open water, but there was no sign of Mara or any of the other Lawless Undine. In fact, there was nothing but floating debris in every direction. I swam toward the horizon, the direction ships normally came from, and finally saw the barge wreckage. A pair of human legs was kicking frantically in the water while one of the Lawless from Mara's clan was circling them, darting in to slash at the man's body with her razor-edged fins. On the last swipe, she wrapped her tail around his legs and tried to pull him under the surface.

I darted to her as fast as I could and pulled her from his back. She saw me and shadowed, disappearing into the dark water below just as a stabbing pain shot through my forearm. I pulled away instinctively, which only seemed to make the pain worse until I stopped, realizing the man was actually *biting* me. I slapped his back with my tail and was free, the flesh on my arm ragged and bleeding as I scanned for anyone else from Mara's clan, and especially for any other halflings.

In the shafts of setting sunlight that shot through the water, it seemed only wooden planks and the bodies of human men who had been stripped nearly bare of their coverings were falling into the dark waters below. The only other Undines weren't far in the distance—a school of them swimming away from the wreckage, some of them halflings like Opal.

But not all of them.

"Dynah!" I echoed through the water to Mara's friend, another Lawless Undine from the Northern Depths. She whipped around when the sound reached her, and a smile peeled across her thin, silver face.

"Your *Highness*?" She didn't bother to retract her needle-like hunting teeth as she glanced at the wound on my arm. Her grin widened. "My, what happened there? Did one of the beasts *bite* you?"

"Did you forget the law, Dynah? The treaty with the Gnome Queen? Undines are *not* to attack the ships!"

"Well, I suppose that depends on what you mean by *attack...*" She lifted a finger to her chin in mock contemplation, her silver hair disappearing, then reappearing in the play of fading light this close to the surface.

I put the trinkets in my hand around my neck and darted behind her to bind her arms with her hair. "Forget it. You can explain it to the queen."

Dynah laughed. "How many more of our kind have to die, Cora? How many more ships should we hide from in fear?"

"*Ask* the queen," I echoed through my teeth as I steered her through the water.

"I see. No more thinking for yourself now that you're about to become captain of her ridiculous guard?"

Oh no...the ceremony... Panic welled in my chest.

"Her *ridiculous* guard keeps us all safe," Reed echoed, appearing in the murky water just ahead of us. "Unlike you, who would send the halflings to their deaths with your uprisings." Reed shot a green glare at me. "And as I was *trying* to say earlier, *Lieutenant*, if you'd ever like *to be* captain, may I suggest we *go* now!?"

"I forgot… I forgot about the ceremony," I stammered, and then lost all the outrage he'd made me feel. "Reed, *your* promotion?"

"We'll both be fashionably late," he echoed, still glaring at me.

Dynah laughed again until I tightened the twist of hair around her arms, and we swam as fast as we could back to the Ring of Fire, a circle of smokestacks that surrounded the Royal Cavern.

*****

Two of the queen's personal guards greeted us, each of them half the size of an orca, complete with winding, spiraling rank tattoos over their silver chests and shoulders.

"Your Highness?" Enoch, the guard on the right bowed.

"*Lieutenant*, please, Enoch," I echoed impatiently, gesturing for him to straighten.

He glanced at Reed and me. "Aren't you supposed to be at the promotion ceremony…*right now*?"

"I know. I just saw three halflings too close to the boundary waters, then discovered they were carrying human goods," I explained. The guards exchanged glances as I held up the chains I'd seized. "*Dynah* brought the humans' boat down. I'm taking her to the queen."

"I did *not* sabotage the boat!" Dynah jerked against her restraints as I pushed her forward, the guards moving to either side.

"Oh, let me guess, it sunk itself?" I shoved her again.

"Yes! That barge belonged to the Gnome Queen, Your *Highness*. And if you think *I'm* the worst of your problems…"

I spun her around to face me. "That was the *Luna Bay*? Mama Luz's barge?"

"That's what I'm telling you!" Dynah's eyes widened, even shadowed for a second at the sound of the Gnome Queen's name.

"At what point did you think it would be a good idea to strip her *dead* sailors and attack the ones still trying to stay afloat in the water?" I raised my forearm in front of her face. "One of them *bit* me when I pulled your minion from his back!"

"We didn't know it was the *Luna Bay* when we started scavenging. The barge just…collapsed."

"Barges don't just *collapse*, especially not that close to shore, Dynah. Why am I even listening to this? Explain it to the queen."

"Could you hold her until after the ceremony?" Reed asked sheepishly. Enoch rolled his eyes.

"Go." Shoal, the other enormous guard nodded as he took Dynah by the wrists and led her away.

Chapter 2

"You had one job today, Cora! One job! And it wasn't boundary water patrol!" Reed's muffled echo was entirely too close to my ear as we sped into the corridor that opened to the Royal Cavern. I appreciated that he talked to me like we'd been friends since infancy and not like I was the princess. But he did tend to be a little dramatic.

"I *told you* I was sorry! And for the record, I didn't ask you to come for me."

"*Really*? You're welcome, by the way. You're right, I didn't *have* to come for you. You could have missed your own *Captain of the Guard* promotion instead!"

Reed's long, silver hair came loose from its binding as he darted ahead of me toward the back entrance of the cavern. He cracked the door with his tail and peeked in, refastening his hair at the nape of his neck with his hands.

"I'm sorry... You're right," I echoed, reluctantly. "Thank you."

He smirked at me, but it didn't displace the scowl on his face. "Thank the Mother... They're still announcing the new second lieutenants. Do you even understand how lucky you are?" He didn't wait for my reply. "Come on."

We swam quickly to the front of the colosseum style rows, weaving our way through the first and second lieutenants. Reed found our squadron, and I took my position at the end.

Dorcus, the queen's herald stood at the edge of the drop stage. Her long, silver body was draped in woven sashes and strings of iridescent shells. The queen herself sat on a throne of whale bones and flowering sea cacti, her pearl breastplate shifting color in the shadow of the royal inker's smokestack. The inker, a small, thin triton dressed in similar woven sashes glared at me as he crossed to the smokestack in the center of the stage and refilled his quills.

"Mara, Undine of The Depths," Dorcus announced as my mother took the opportunity to narrow her wide, yellow eyes at me. "Her Royal Majesty, Queen Necksa, bestows upon you the rank of Squadron Captain. Present yourself for promotion."

"Mara!?" I echoed abruptly, turning a few heads in my row. Mara smirked at me as she pushed past. I looked over at Reed, who rightly should have had that promotion, but he didn't so much as blink.

My mother's gaze bore through my chest. I could already hear the scolding about appearances, about how it was a conflict of interest to allow me to serve in the militia when I was the princess, despite me making it perfectly clear to her I only asked to be *one* of these things.

"Cora!" Reed hissed when I realized Dorcus was staring at me, pitching a white eyebrow.

She cleared her throat. "Lieutenant Cora of The Shallows…?"

"Yes, sorry. *Sorry.*" I fumbled, darting quickly down the aisle and to the stage. My mother wouldn't look at me when I finally made it to the master inker.

"Do you accept your new position as Regiment Captain, Cora of The Shallows?" Dorcus asked, her head covered in a woven net of pearls.

"I do," I answered, turning my shoulder to the inker. He removed the quill from the mouth of the smokestack where it had been inserted and refilled it with ink.

I pulled a drag of water through my gills as the master inker tattooed another swirled line over the two already on my arm. The burning travelled down the rest of my arm and numbed everything as I curled my fingers into a fist.

"I pronounce you Regiment Captain, Cora of The Shallows," my mother echoed, the angles of her narrow, silver face creating shadows under her sharp cheekbones. She looked like a phantom floating there behind the smokestack, her long, silver body draped in sashes and shells and wrapped in dissipating smoke.

"Thank you, Your Majesty," I echoed.

"Citizens of The Shallows, I give you our new Captain of the Queen's Guard," my mother echoed, motioning for me to face the gathered crowd when I didn't move. I turned to a harmonized wave of echoes as she spoke again. "Thank you for your attendance at this year's promotion ceremony." My mother began to follow her entourage off the stage as the crowd dispersed.

"Wait!" I called to her. "What about Reed?"

Dorcus stopped and turned to me. "What about him?" The lines around her pinched mouth deepened as she forced a smile.

"He was supposed to be Squadron Captain. How could she have promoted *Mara*?"

"Mara of The Depths has accepted the position," Dorcus answered, but that *wasn't* the question I asked.

I glared at her. "*Mara*!? She's not half as qualified as Reed!" I echoed, louder this time so it would reach down the corridor. "Mother, you must—"

"I must have a squadron leader who is *prompt*," she echoed without stopping or even turning to face me.

"That was my fault!" I called after her. "He was late because he came to get *me* for the ceremony!"

Dorcus looked at me with a laugh in her eyes. "I'm afraid it's done, Your *Highness*."

"Take my promotion back then. He was only late because of *me*."

"We couldn't possibly," Dorcus echoed, a small laugh actually escaping her. She turned to join my mother and her departing entourage.

"Why?"

"Your Majesty?" she looked over her shoulder at me in surprise. "Because you are the *Princess.*"

I wanted to echo loudly enough to rattle the cavern walls, but nothing came out when I opened my mouth. I watched Dorcus leave the cavern.

"It's all right," Reed echoed just beyond the stage. "Mara will be…just fine as Squadron Captain."

"You must be joking. She's the last person who should have any authority. This isn't over. Come on," I echoed, darting through the water of the cavern after my mother.

Shoal, the guard who escorted Dynah to a holding cell, was talking with my mother in the distance by the time I rounded the corner. I sped up before he told her whatever nonsense Dynah had fed him, and Shoal caught my eyes. He nodded to me and moved back from my mother.

She raised a white eyebrow at me. "Cora… What's this about a barge?"

"Where's Dynah?" I echoed to Shoal.

"In her cell, Your Highness."

"*Please* stop calling me that!"

We followed the towering guard around a few more limestone corners before we arrived at Dynah's cell. She was sharpening her nails on the stone wall, which just made me angrier for some reason.

"Your Highness." She forced a smile when she saw us.

My mother cleared her throat and folded her arms over her armored breastplate. "Ah, Dynah of The Depths. And why are you bound in my detainment cell?"

"Surely, Your Majesty was aware of the assault that took place just beyond the boundary waters? One of our own, again, hurt by *humans*," she echoed innocently.

My mother narrowed her eyes, concerned, then looked to me for answers. I could only shake my head. Dynah hadn't told me one of the Undines had been hurt.

"What assault?" I echoed, glaring at her.

"On *you*, of course, Your Highness." She glanced at my arm.

"What? *This*?" I raised my forearm and glanced at the bite wound. "No, this is because—" I started, but she cut me off.

"And I've already shown Cora the attack on the Gnome Queen's barge, Your Majesty. In *our* waters, no less. Mara has learned that the Gnome Queen believes it was us rather than her own mutinous crew."

I gasped involuntarily at the ridiculousness of the claim.

"Were there survivors?" My mother looked intently from Dynah to me. "And the Gnome Queen? Has there been any sight of her?"

"I… I didn't see her, Mother. There was only—"

"Send an envoy to the boundary waters." She interrupted me. "Search everywhere. She must be found. Bring any survivors to the shore. We cannot afford anything that looks like we've broken the treaty."

"Oh, it's too late for that," Dynah echoed innocently. I wanted to murder her with her own hair. "They're all dead. And those of us who even *tried* to help the sailors were met with violence. Just look at Cora's arm."

I'd already forgotten again about the bite the human inflicted when I'd pulled the halfling from his back. I looked down and noticed the wound was still ragged, and the pain started all over again.

My mother blanched and looked at my arm. "A human did this to you when you tried to *help* him?"

I stammered. "Well, no. I mean, yes, but it just happened so fast," I finished idiotically, like that ridiculous statement alone would somehow negate the fury in my mother's darkening eyes.

"I see. Cora, go to the infirmary." The queen nodded to Shoal. "And you see that Dynah is released."

"No!" I caught myself before I continued. "Dynah was *leading* the halflings to raid the wreckage. It was probably Mara's idea! Look!" I pulled the chains from around my neck and held them out to her.

"I'm afraid we have bigger problems than this now. *Captain*, see to your wound and then assemble a team to find the Gnome Queen. Dynah, thank you for reporting this. You're free to go."

"*What?* Mother!" I began to protest, but Dynah stopped me with an obnoxious, sweeping bow.

"Of course, Your Majesty. I'm at your service," she lied as Shoal unlocked the cell door.

I started to protest again, but it was pointless in the wake of everyone's departure and Reed's untimely entrance.

"That looks bad" he echoed, glancing at my arm. "I didn't realize you'd been *bitten*, Cora."

He tried to cradle my elbow with his arm, but I pushed him back squarely in the chest. "I could've used your corroboration on what happened out there. Dynah has my mother thinking the humans mutinied and sunk their own barge, but that Mama Luz will blame us since it happened near in our waters!" I echoed.

None of this seemed to get through to Reed. "We can deal with that after you go to the infirmary. We can't do anything if you get a blood infection."

"Reed, are you listening to me? Mara's clan attacked that barge. There were men still alive who *saw* the Undines attacking—maybe even Mama Luz herself!"

"Cora, let go, you're—"

"It's a clear law to stay away from the humans! They blatantly disregard—"

"Cora!" he echoed loudly, startling me into silence.

"*What?*"

Reed cupped the fist I had wrapped around the chains and lifted my arm, which was bleeding all over again.

"Infirmary? I don't want to have to kill any innocent sharks today just because you're stubborn."

Chapter 3

I'd almost let myself forget about Reed losing his promotion to Squadron Captain all because of me. The realization of it washed through me again like sand in my gills, and I instinctively swallowed hard to combat the feeling.

It didn't work.

"Reed, I'm sorry about your promotion. I didn't mean to—"

"Don't worry about it," he echoed as we left the infirmary, my arm wrapped in kelp and covered by a piece of mollusk shell. "You should really wait here for the healer, though."

"We don't have time. She'd make me sit through a saline infusion since this is a human bite, and we need to find at least some of the squadron to look for Mama Luz."

We swam through the now-empty Royal Cavern and out the corridor to the open water. I had no idea where my squadron—er, Mara's squadron was now with everyone scattered after the promotions ceremony, that is, until I saw Dynah wrapping herself around three of my—of *Mara's*—new second lieutenants.

Reed laughed. "Found some of the squadron."

I rolled my eyes and swam toward them.

"Oh, Your *Highness*..." Dynah bowed obnoxiously.

"Save it," Reed echoed. "We need to find Mama Luz. *Now.* And you're going to show us where she is."

Dynah's silver skin flickered in shades of gray and black at the mention of the Gnome Queen's name. The three-second lieutenants stood at attention, the fins just below their jawlines fanned straight out.

"Stand down," Mara echoed, waving to the lieutenants as she approached. Her silver hair was pulled tightly against her scalp, her new Squadron Captain bar tattoo on her shoulder red and angry. "We have no idea where to find the Gnome Queen. She probably washed up on that island and is plotting her invasion as we speak."

"We're under the queen's orders to find her, and Dynah is going to beg her forgiveness for sinking her barge." I glared at her. "I know you ordered that attack, Mara."

She laughed so loudly that the reverberation actually rang in my ears.

"Scan the shore," Reed echoed to the young lieutenants. "We'll be right behind you."

They nodded, fanning the fins below their jaws one more time in acknowledgement before disappearing into the dark waters toward the island.

"Take us to the Gnome Queen, Mara," I echoed, extending my arm for her to lead the way. She cocked a silver eyebrow at me and smiled just before exchanging glances with Dynah and together, darted away. "Mara!"

We moved quickly through the water and around the coral reef just before the boundary line that separated our territory from the open water—from the depths of the lawless Undines like Dynah who were still subject to my mother's rule, but did not respect it. Ships were dragged down there without a trace remaining, despite our laws against interfering with anything above the skim.

"Cora! Let them go!" Reed called to me.

"They need to answer for what they did!"

We chased Mara and Dynah into the depths, the moonlight diluting in the water the farther out we went. It was still and surreal with only jellyfish floating by periodically until Mara finally slowed, then darted behind a dune. Dynah was right behind her.

"We're too far from the boundary, Cora. Let them go," Reed insisted again. A great white shark moved slowly in the distance beyond the dune, and the phosphorous algae on the skim created a soft, eerie blue canopy under the moonlight. I swam after Mara, ignoring Reed's protests, then stopped abruptly when I rounded the corner.

"Your Highness!" Opal echoed, her long, silver hair instantly shadowing in fear.

"Opal? What in the seven seas...?" I started, but didn't need to finish my question when I saw the sneer on Mara's silver, almost glowing face. She swam a half-circle around Opal, gathering her into the group of five other Undines of The Depths: Dynah, two other sirens, and two tritons, each of them glowing arrogantly. Their silver hair mottled in the light, and their round, dark eyes bore into me. They smiled, revealing four rows of small, sharp, needle-like teeth.

"Is this Cora, Princess of the Undines?" one of the tritons asked. "Out slumming are you, Your *Highness*?" he moved slowly toward me, swimming in a circle around me.

Reed drew the short spear from his sling. "Know your place, triton."

Mara smiled. "Oh, Lieutenant. We're all friends here, aren't we, Opal?" She stroked Opal's hair, which was shifting from silver to black.

"Why are you *here*, Opal?" I echoed as calmly as I could. All five of the Lawless Undines circled us.

"I'm sorry, Your Highness. Please don't put me in the hole," she echoed, flickering with fear.

Mara continued to pet Opal's color-shifting hair. "She won't put you anywhere, halfling. Don't worry. Our friend will be here soon."

I narrowed my eyes at Mara. "What *friend*?"

The disturbance in the water came first—the low, reverberating hum of ship engines.

"It's another ship," Reed echoed, surprised. "No, *two* ships."

I glared at Mara. "What are you planning out here? Another attack? The queen won't tolerate this. As Captain of the Guard, I officially charge you with treason, Mara. You're going to the hole."

I advanced to bind her arms, but she moved too quickly, twisting and wrapping Opal's long, silver hair around the halfling's neck until she was clawing to free her gills.

"I don't think so, *Princess*. You as Captain of the Guard will be no different from you as Squadron Captain. You're really just a pampered little pearl who has no idea about the real world. We're done waiting for you to lead."

I lunged at her, stopping only when Opal's strangled voice halted me. The two tritons attacked Reed, one lashing at his arms and the other cutting his torso with his razored fins while another siren went for his throat. I pulled my short spear from the sheath and hit Mara in the face, catching it in her hair and jerking her away from Reed. I jabbed the other end of the spear into the closest triton's ribs, which gave Reed enough space to pin his remaining attacker's throat to the dune with the center of his spear.

"Come here, Opal," I commanded, pulling my spear free from the siren's hair and holding it ready in case anyone decided to attack again.

Mara gripped Opal's hair. "You don't own the Undine, *Your Highness*."

"Stop *calling* me that!" I darted toward her, and she raced up the dune pulling Opal through the skim to the surface. "Opal!" I echoed, breaking through to the open air. I couldn't see either of them in the sparkle of moonlight over the water...or over the shadows of approaching ships.

The sandbar stretched for as far as I could see in front of me. The ships would be forced to come directly through this channel. Directly toward *us*, which was exactly where they were headed. Mara did this on purpose. She led us here.

Reed surfaced next to me along with the other three Undines, who laughed collectively, but no longer tried to attack us.

"Where's Opal?" he echoed.

"Mara took her over the dune."

Reed noticed the sandbar and sheathed his spear. "Into the cove?"

"No, they'd be cut off from the depths there." I echoed. "She wouldn't risk that. She has to be—"

"Right in front of you," Dynah echoed through a laugh. Mara was swimming toward the approaching ship, her tail and Opal's both disappearing into the water.

"No!" I echoed, hearing my voice like a human's shriek above the water. I dove under through the skim after them, my spear catching in the seaweed field and ripping stalks from their roots, which slowed me down. Reed shot in front of me in pursuit of Opal, and soon, we were both free of the field.

The Lawless Undine surfaced and dove like dolphins triangulating the two boats—the first one much smaller than the second. They echoed location signals, and within minutes, dozens of Lawless were encircling the crafts.

Reed swam to my side. "There are too many Lawless, Cora. We won't be able to stop them if they attack."

"I know. We just need to get Opal and return to The Shallows. We're too far out now for any of the Guard to hear a rally echo."

Reed and I swam toward Mara and Opal while the Lawless were taunting the men aboard the boats. Some of them succumbed to the echoes that sounded like birdsongs above the skim and leaped over their deck railings. Once in the water, they were quickly surrounded by the Lawless, whose birdsong echoes became background shrieking to the cries of the drowning men.

"Opal! Come with us! This isn't what you want! This isn't who you are!" I echoed to her, but she was already completely shadowed in Mara's grasp, her hair, her skin, even her eyes pulsing black with fear.

"And what are deez here ya brought me?" a voice called down from the railing of the smaller ship. It came from a woman in red, her braided black hair stacked on top of her head and wrapped in a red cloth. She flashed a wide, white smile that ripped a hole in the moonlit air. *The Gnome Queen.*

"It's her," Reed echoed, his voice above the skim sounding rough and low.

"Is dat da wee princess?" Mama Luz asked, squinting in my direction.

"Oh, she doesn't like being called that now. She's *Captain of the Guard*," Mara answered mockingly.

Mama Luz raised both her dark eyebrows, the whites of her eyes standing out that much more against her dark skin.

"Is it dat way now den? All righty, Miss Captain of de Guard. Come, come to me child. Let me see how you've grown."

Mama Luz waved me toward the barge, which was *not* the Luna Bay. Behind her, more splashes and screams filled the night air, causing Opal to start squalling until Mara wrapped Opal's hair over her mouth.

"Let her go!" I echoed to Mara, pulling my short spear out of the sheath again.

"Tsk, tsk," Mama Luz said. "At least, not among yer own kind. But dat's entirely up to you now, ain't it?"

"You weren't on the Luna Bay when it sank?" I asked, but I didn't get an answer before a man started yelling to one of the sailors who was lowering a smaller boat to the water.

"Pull him up! That's an order!" the man shouted, but only some of the others were listening. Once the boat hit the skim, the man inside leaned over the edge to reach for the female Undines who were tempting him, floating on their backs and pulling at their chest wraps, their echoes blending together in a chorus that had the man nearly falling from the boat.

Other Undine swam to him, pulling at his coverings until he was free of them. With outstretched arms, one of the Undine came close enough to him to be half-lifted into his boat. He embraced her, pressing his face to her body, to her mouth, until she opened her jaws and swallowed his head, pulling the rest of his coverless body into the water where the rest of her clan devoured him in a frenzy of splashes and shrieking.

"Stop! Stop, I command you all in the name of the queen!" I echoed, but none of them obeyed.

"Aw, little princess. Dey not gonna listen to ya, urchin," Mama Luz said. "Dis boat is der payment."

"Payment for what?" Reed demanded over my shoulder.

"Ah, he's a handsome one. I may keep dat one for me-self."

"You brought that boat here?" I asked. "You brought it to the Lawless so they could attack it?"

"Well, of course I did. I need happy allies in dis war, now don't I?"

I shook my head at her, confused. "We're not at war... We have the treaty!"

Mama Luz threw her head back in a booming laugh. "Not wit you all, child. Don't yer mama tell you nothin'?

We takin' back our world, Princess. Takin' it back from de human beasts. Jest look at dem," she said, gesturing in disgust at the men pulling at their coverings and climbing over themselves to get into the small boats that were lowering to the skim.

They grabbed at the taunting Undines, occasionally pulling them up into the boat by their hair in the seconds before the men's flesh was torn from their bones.

"I want to go home!" Opal shrieked at the sight and bolted from Mara's grasp. Blocked by the sandbar behind us, she darted into the open water...directly toward the boats.

Chapter 4

"No, Opal! Not that way!" Reed called, and we both dove after her. She was faster than we were, but she couldn't navigate the falling bodies and darting Lawless ravaging them. She swam directly into a lowered net, which was quickly lifting out of the water.

"Opal!" I echoed, swimming toward it to cut her free. It pulled us both out of the water and onto the deck of the largest ship where several men were waiting with their teeth bared. Opal struggled in the net as I tried to cut her free with the edge of my short spear, her screeches causing the men to cover their ears.

"Get back to your posts!" one of the men commanded. His coverings were different from the other men. White and ornately woven. His dark hair was tied like Reed's, and his blue eyes were stormy with rage like the most violent of seas.

"But Captain, lookee what we caught. A harpy!"

Opal shrieked again as the men grabbed at her, only tightening herself in the net.

"I said get back to your posts! We're under attack, you fools!" the man in the ornate coverings...*the captain,* shouted, pulling out a blade and cutting the net.

"She looks like a lassie! Git me that harpy lassie!" one of the men said.

"We got two! And this one's ripe!" another man said, pulling the net tight around my arms and making me drop my spear. He pulled off my armor plate, and I bit him, ripping the flesh from his arm. He screamed and fell back.

Two of the other men rushed me just as the captain slashed the net entangling Opal. She pulled herself to my side, which stopped the advancing men for a second. They laughed.

"It's a momma and lassie, mates!"

"Nah, the ripe one ain't ripe enough for a lassie that old!"

"Since when do you know the breedings of harpies, ya dolt! Make room, mates!" one of the men said, grabbing Opal's arm.

A blade came through the man's shoulder, and then back out as he fell over Opal's tail. She shrieked and clung to my arms as he scrambled.

"Pull my spear from the sheath, Opal. Do it now!" I echoed, but she couldn't get to it before the captain started walking toward us, blade in hand.

"You were right, Your Highness! I'm sorry. I'm sorry I didn't obey you!"

"It's all right, Opal," I replied, then whipped my tail under the captain's legs. If he wanted to take our lives, he would have to do it from his knees.

One of the other men lunged at us, and I knocked him over the railing with a second whip. The captain got to his feet and raised his blade over me.

"Opal! Close your eyes!" I echoed as the blade came down…severing the weave of the net binding my arms. I shook free of it and looked at the man, who had his hand to his head, rubbing it.

"Go! Take her, and go," he said, waving us toward the water as he turned to slash another man who lunged at us. That man fell over my tail fin, and I flung him over the railing.

The captain continued fighting the men who would have otherwise swarmed us. I grabbed Opal around the waist and sprang over the railing, piercing the skim and diving below the fray of humans being massacred by the Lawless Undines.

We swam back to the sandbar and found Mama Luz's barge still there, but Mara and those from her clan were gone. I had to find Reed.

"I'm sorry, Your Highness. I'm sorry! This is all my fault!" Opal cried, her airborne voice sounding like a distant birdcall.

"It's not. It may not even be Mara's if Mama Luz brought that boat through here. What did Mara tell you?"

"Only that the Gnome Queen didn't just want peace with us. She wanted an alliance."

I shook my head, confused. "Why? Against what?"

"The humans."

"Cora!" Reed echoed, swimming toward us.

"Thank the Mother. We need to get back to the queen," I echoed, but then I heard Mara echoing in pain. "Take Opal back to The Shallows. Tell my mother the Gnome Queen isn't waging war on us. She's waging it on the humans, and the Lawless are helping her."

"Where are you going!?"

"To help Mara."

I shoved Opal into his arms and swam away before he could protest, following Mara's distress echo that had since turned to one of anger. I answered it, telling her to be calm, that I was coming to help.

I followed it back toward the larger boat, where Opal and I had been pulled up in the dragnet. The bodies of men were still falling from the railing, struggling in the water until they were stripped and drowned, devoured, in some cases, while they were still screaming.

I broke the surface of the skim and saw Mara at the base of the boat clutching her shoulder, which had been slashed. Still, she tried climbing the dragnet that was draped over the side of the boat. On the deck, the one they'd called *Captain* who had fought off the men advancing on Opal and me, was desperately struggling to stop the men from pulling up the net…and Mara.

"She will kill you, too, you fools!" he shouted to them. He was quickly becoming outnumbered, so he strategically started to cut the dragnet with his blade. It became entangled in one of the upstrokes, and Mara did not miss her opportunity. She jerked the net, and the captain flew over the railing into the water.

"No… Mara, no!"

I swam toward them, dodging the fallen bodies and the gnashing Undine until I was in the middle of their struggle. The captain held Mara at bay by her throat, but his grip would not hold for long as she slashed at his arms with her razor-edged fins. It seemed like he'd drown rather than release her.

He didn't understand my commands, and Mara was no longer able to obey them even if she wanted to with his hand around her throat. I had to separate them. I had to get him away from her…from all the Undine.

I launched myself at his torso and pulled him from her, shooting through the water so quickly, he couldn't fight the current. By the time we reached the island of The Shallows, the shore where the Luna Bay had sunk, he was unconscious.

I swam as far as I could onto the shore without risking beaching myself. The water lapped all around us, pushing his dark hair from his face.

"Can you hear me?" I echoed. He stirred, opening his eyes only for a brief moment.

"You?" he whispered before falling unconscious again.

I didn't know his language completely, but I'd studied enough of it to know he was never trying to hurt Opal or me. Not like the others. He didn't deserve to die like they did, although I felt guilty for believing that as well. I needed to get back to my mother to tell her of the war. I needed to tell Reed what the Gnome Queen was planning, and we needed to assemble the Guard. None of this would happen while I lay here in the splashing surf next to this human. This captain. A captain of his own guard.

A warrior. Like me.

***

He was breathing, so I let the tide pull me back toward the rocks, then past them and into The Shallows. I watched the captain lay there until the first rays of sunlight fell over him, and when he finally coughed himself awake, I dove under the skim.

Every joint, every muscle in my body ached, and the burns on my tail from the rope had gone numb in the saltwater. The mollusk shell covering the bite wound on my arm had cracked and dug into my forearm, causing another series of cuts and scrapes. This time, I might just let Reed talk me into waiting for the healer at the infirmary.

But when I got back to the Royal Cavern, no one was there.

"Mother?" I echoed. When she didn't answer, panic rose in my chest. *Where had everyone gone?* "Enoch! Shoal!" I echoed again for her guards, but they didn't answer me either. I left the Cavern and swam to the barracks to find the Guard, but they, too, were empty. Everything was in order just as it had been at the Cavern. It was just...deserted. "Reed!"

"Your Highness..." the halfling's voice echoed. It was coming from *the hole* of all places.

"Opal?" I echoed back, swimming quickly to unlatch the small door to the stone cave next to the barracks.

Opal was curled into the corner, darting out like a striking eel when she saw me. She threw her arms around me and wailed.

"I knew you'd come!" she echoed.

"Where is Reed? Where is *everyone*?"

"Reed took me to the queen and told her what happened with Mara and the Lawless Undines," she echoed, nearly choking on the words and shifting from silver to black.

"It's all right, Opal. Just relax."

"He told her they needed to evacuate The Shallows because of the Gnome Queen and what happened with the boats," she echoed quickly. "He insisted that they go while he went after you."

"But then why weren't you with the evacuation? Why were you in the hole?" I asked.

"I just wanted to help. I slipped away from the Queen's Guards so I could follow Reed. I just wanted to help him, but they discovered me."

"*Who*, Opal?"

"Mara and the Lawless. They took him to the Gnome Queen."

"Where? Back to the sandbar?"

"Yes, onto her boat. He told me to swim…to hide. I didn't know where to go, so I came here, but then that door closed behind me, and I was so scared…" she trailed off in sobs.

"All right, it's all right now, Opal. Listen to me. The Guard would have led the evacuation to the Southern Depths. We have allies there, but it's too dangerous to go without a school. Your parents must be frantic."

"I'm sorry…I just wanted to help. The others wouldn't have caught him if I'd have listened."

"It's all right, Opal. Reed is a soldier. He'll be all right," I echoed, both to assure the halfling and myself. "*I* need your help now. I need you to be a little soldier. Can you do that for me?"

She looked up at me soberly, the mottled pulse of her silver and black hair stabilizing to a muted gray. She nodded. "What should I do?"

"Be brave, Opal. And stay close to me."

Chapter 5

We reached the boundary waters only to find the Lawless Undines replaced by a frenzy of sharks, the larger boat destroyed and half-sunken. It would be completely submerged by sunset to be sure. The tide would clear away the scraps of the ship that would not sink, and the sharks would clear away the scraps of men.

The smaller boat Mama Luz was on was also still anchored near the sand bar, but it, too, seemed abandoned.

"Where did they all go?" Opal echoed as we broke the surface of the water. Her voice a thin birdsong in the open air.

I scanned around the sandbar, where there were only more sharks and scavenger fish. No Undines and no Mama Luz.

"Are you sure this is where they took Reed?"

Opal nodded adamantly. "Four Lawless tritons did it. They wrapped him in the rope the crew threw down. Mara and Dynah wanted to go too, but Mama Luz told them they knew there was only room for one more. That's when…" she trailed off.

"Opal, what is it? That's when *what* happened?"

"That's when Mara killed her."

"She killed the Gnome Queen!?"

"No! She killed Dynah," Opal sobbed and looked quickly over the sandbar. "She sliced her throat and threw her to the sharks in the cove…just there."

"Sacred Mother…" I was hesitant to press for more details, but I needed to know what happened to Reed. "Opal, did Mara get on that ship?"

She shook her head. "No, Mama Luz told her to finish off the boat she'd brought us. She told the four Lawless tritons to go after they tied up Reed, and for Mara to follow them." She sobbed harder, and her skin started to shadow. "The tritons left, but Mara wouldn't go with them. She tried to cut Reed's ropes, and that's when Mama Luz had her crew pull him up."

"This boat?" I gestured to the one in front of us.

"Yes." Opal tried to breathe the air, but her gills kept flaring with her uncontrolled sobs and she choked.

"All right, calm down. The boat is still here, right? Reed must be aboard." I stroked Opal's hair until the black finally faded. "Come with me."

I dove under the boat and pressed my cheek to the bottom of the hull. There was no trace of Reed's echo, so I sounded one of my own and listened.

"I don't hear him," Opal echoed, her expression falling.

"Just follow me."

We swam under the boat to the other side, my short spear in hand. I surfaced quietly, just enough for my eyes to clear the skim, and I nearly splashed when I saw Reed bound in rope from his chest to halfway down his tail. His head was hanging forward, and my stomach dropped.

"There he is!" Opal chirped above the water, which startled him. All in the same second I was both flooded with relief that he was alive and panic that someone else had heard Opal.

"Go! It's a trap!" Reed said, his airborne echo sounding like a screaming hawk. I dove for Opal and pulled her past the underside of the boat, the net that came up all around me just missing her. I cut a hole wide enough to fall through with my short spear, hoping I would fall to the water, but I landed on the barge deck instead of back in the sea.

Reed was dropped next to me, and I quickly cut his ropes, but something was wrong. His silver hair was yellowed and his pale skin covered in a white film that was cracking. He didn't move right away after I cut his ropes. I gripped my short spear ready to fight, but there were no sailors poised to attack. There was nothing for several seconds until we heard the rolling, disembodied laughter of a woman I couldn't find. She was just... *everywhere.*

"It's her..." Reed said, but his voice above the water sounded squeezed and breathless. "It's Luz..."

She appeared from below deck, rising out of the dark entrance slowly but steadily toward us.

"What do you want from us!?" I shouted to her, but the sound of my voice was pitched and wordless—a series of sharp screams like a diving waterbird.

Mama Luz laughed again, this time, with pity. "Oh, child. You gonna draw dem gulls to peck yer bones." She waved a hand at me, and my throat immediately tightened. I coughed as the constriction increased, the gills under my jawline pinching, stretching until I was sure she was somehow strangling me. I clutched at the invisible hands, but the only thing I felt was my own throat. My gills were…*gone*.

Reed screeched like a wounded bird, but Mama Luz just laughed even harder, drowning him out.

"Nooo!" I yelled, and this time, I heard the *word*. I heard my voice, but it wasn't like a hungry gull's anymore. It was *human*.

"Now, dat's better," Mama Luz said. I felt again for my gills, finding only rough patches of skin that were already peeling in their place. "Listen to me, girl. Yer fishy-man ain't long fa yer world," she added, raising her thin, black eyebrows.

"He needs…the water!" I coughed, clutching my throat again, which felt like I'd swallowed sand.

Mama Luz returned her dark eyes to me. "*Yes*, he do. But whedder he go back to it or not be up to you, me urchin."

I nodded furiously, and the Gnome Queen just threw her head back in another wave of laughter, her black braids flying in all directions from under her red head scarf.

"Let him go!" I coughed again.

"All righty. I put him in de water, but only if ya help me wit a little problem," she finally managed, her laughter dying off.

"Don't…" Reed called to me, his voice even thinner than before.

Mama Luz clapped her hand, summoning two dark-skinned men with wide, jaundiced eyes. "Bring up da buckets and toss 'em on dis little fishy, me loves."

Neither of the men spoke. They only nodded and tied a stretch of rope to two metal pails, then tossed them over the railing. They pulled them up full of water and emptied them both on Reed. He gasped, his gills flaring, and the silver sheen of his skin reappeared.

"Don't...worry about me, Cora. Don't trust her!" His airborne voice stronger, again like a hawk or an eagle screaming through the sky.

"Aww, hush, now. See de gratitude I git, little princess?"

"What do you want from us?" I glared at her.

Mama Luz smiled widely. "I got me a little exchange in de works wit yer sister, see?"

"*Mara?* She is *not* my sister," I said loudly even though it burned my throat to do it.

Mama Luz just shrugged. "She want dat human you skittered away wit gone like de rest on dat gift boat I brought."

"Cora, don't!" Reed coughed again, forcing himself to breathe the air.

"I told her, fine. I send me gnomes out to drag him back to de water, and you know what she said to dat?" Mama Luz's dark eyes widened. "She squeaked at me, *oh no, no, no...it got to be de princess dat kills him since she swam him away.*"

"*Kill* him?" I whispered. "Mara is delusional, and so are you if you think I'm going to kill anyone!"

Mama Luz's smile withered. "You either be killin' dat son of Eve you swam to da shore or you be killin' dis man-fishy here," she said, reaching toward Reed, and without touching him, she pulled her fingers into a fist.

Reed began violently gasping, even though he was nowhere close to her.

"Stop!" I shouted, my human voice strong, but painful to use, but she only kept squeezing his throat. "All right! Just let him go!"

Mama Luz's wide, red smile returned. "Dat's more like it den," she said, releasing Reed. He leaned back gasping and coughing. "All right, now. Let's see 'bout dis tail… You jes keep still."

She opened her palms and held them out at me. My stomach began to turn and a sharp pain started in my back, running down the length of my tail until I thought it might rip in two, which is *exactly* what it did.

The burning sensation intensified as the scales charred and peeled away, disappearing into ash that blew away in the breeze. Underneath were two pale human legs that moved independently from one another.

I pushed back from them without thinking, only to see them helping me—they kicked and pushed as if they had a mind of their own. It took several seconds to realize they were part of me. Part of *my* body.

My dorsal fin was gone…the fins on my forearms, gone." What did you do to me?" I gasped.

Mama Luz laughed. "You can't go floppin' onto da beach like a seal now, child." Mama Luz laughed as she threw me a long piece of cloth and pointed to my legs. "Dis is a *skirt*. Bend de knees right der and put dem feets in da smaller hole, den pull de whole ting up. Can't go ashore wit yer naturals all about. Humans are funny about der naturals." She grinned.

I did as she said, pulling the covering up over my chest as I sat on the ground. I pushed the...*knees* of the legs together and flattened the feet on the deck, but I couldn't rise. Mama Luz laughed again and moved toward me, her arm extended to me.

"Put Reed back in the water..." I glared at her as I took her hand. My teeth started to chatter, and she gave me a pitiful look.

"We put him in de cage until ya do yer part." Mama Luz nodded to two of her crew, who stepped forward from the shadows and dragged him into an iron cage.

"He'll die in there!" I yelled, my voice loud and shrill. "He needs the *ocean*!"

"Don't fret, child! We gonna lower dat over de side a de boat...for at least a little while each day." Mama Luz laughed as she took a jar from her shoulder bag and smudged some of the white powder it held over my lips and face, then over my neck and chest before she blew a cloud of it at me. "Ya jes worry 'bout yer part now. I give ya tree days to make dat captain kiss ya of his own free will, and when dat powder make him fall dead for doin' it, you spill his dead man's blood in da water and dive in after it," she said, sprinkling the rest of the white powder into the sea. "Da water will make ya Undine again. Ya come back here as yer natural self, and we open de cage fer yer fishy love."

I opened my mouth to say something else, to protest or negotiate more, but two of her crew were already lifting me up and half carrying me to the little boat hanging on the side of the barge.

"Wait!" I finally yelled. "What if I can't find the captain?"

Mama Luz laughed low in her throat. "We bring you to where he is, don'cha fret none."

"But what if I can't kill him?"

"Den de earth will see ya, water child. It will see you and de fishy-man," she said with a low, rolling laugh.

"What does that mean?" I called after her, but she only laughed louder. "Mama Luz! What does that mean!?"

Her crewmen dumped me into the lifeboat, one of them climbing in and grabbing the paddles while the other lowered the boat to the water. I saw Opal circling below and hoped she would get clear. We hit the water with a splash, and I breathed a sigh of relief to see her dorsal fin cutting through the skim. She swam next to the boat until she suddenly veered wide and surfaced.

"Cora!" she called. Her airborne voice pitched and sharp.

"I'll get Reed back, Opal! Mara set up the trap, but I'll get him back!"

"But where are you going?" she sang.

"Ashore, to get what Mama Luz wants in exchange for Reed. Go back to The Shallows before my mother's group gets too far! Catch up and go with them to the Southern Depths to find your parents!"

"When are you coming back? Cora!" she chirped one last time, then glanced at the sun just peeking over the horizon as it vanished beneath the skim. I didn't have the chance to tell her not to be afraid, for it would not really turn her to stone.

Chapter 6

We rowed into a thick fog that rose around the island, the reflecting sun forcing me to squint. It seemed like time stood still while we passed through it, but on the other side, nothing was the same.

The island was gone. In place of the thick forest were huge, gray structures growing from the earth. There were only a few small trees, and several boats sitting in a row against the shore.

The crewman who had been rowing us abruptly turned around and grabbed my arm.

"Stop! Let me go!" I tried pulling from his grip, but he was too strong. He stood in the center of the boat and pulled me with him, then tossed me overboard. "Wait! This isn't where I left the captain!" Without a word, he sat again and began to row away, watching me until he disappeared into the fog.

It took me the better part of the morning to walk without falling. I walked along the shore looking out at the sky, the sparse trees, the endless stretch of stone towers that rose from the earth. Gulls flew overhead and dove at the water. Their calls wrenched my heart because they sounded like Opal's airborne voice. She would be on her way to the Southern Deep now with the others. With my mother and the Royal Guard. With *Mara*, unless she somehow managed to stay behind, circling like a shark around Mama Luz's barge.

"You are unregistered," a man's voice said, but there was no man to be seen. I looked again in the direction of the voice and saw only a silver cube with a bright light pointing at me. Another cube appeared at its side.

"You are unregistered. State your census number," I heard again, and I finally realized the voices were coming *from* these cubes.

"I'm looking for the captain," I said, but this only made the cubes approach me. "Do you know where I can find him?"

"You are unregistered," the voice said again, but I couldn't be sure which of the two cubes was talking. "State your census number."

"I don't know what that is… Wait!" I shouted as one of the cubes shone a light on me that encircled my waist, somehow pinning my arms to my sides. "What is this?" I tried to move, but I couldn't.

"You are unauthorized," the voice repeated as the cubes turned, the light *lifting* me off the ground.

We moved quickly over the gray terrain until we stopped at one of the tall structures. The cubes took me through an opening, where inside, a woman glanced at me, then pushed a circle on the shelf in front of her. A cage made of glowing bars flickered for a second in the corner as the cubes steered me toward them, and the flickering stopped—the strong, orange glow of the electricity making my skin prickle as they set me down inside the bars.

"All right, where you from, sister?" the woman asked. Her coverings were black, and her skin was dark like the crewmen's on Mama Luz's barge. Her eyes were bright and expressive, though, so I knew she couldn't be one of Mama Luz's minions.

"*Sister*?" I asked.

She raised a dark eyebrow at me and blew out a breath. "Not from The Grind, then," she said to the panel in front of her. "You can't be from The Citadel or you'd be chipped. What's that on your neck? You have your chip taken out?"

"*Chip*?"

"Your census chip—keeps track of how many years you owe, hello?"

I shook my head, still not sure what she meant. "Hello," I replied, though the greeting seemed a little late if you asked me.

"Funny. Did you get some hack to remove your chip or not?"

"I don't know…what that is," I stammered.

The woman closed her eyes in a long blink. "The chip that keeps track of your debt. You pay with time from your *life*, hours, minutes, days, months, years, you understand? What kind of accent is that? You from overseas or something?"

"The Sea? Yes, I'm from the sea!" Finally, something that made sense.

"*Greaaaat*," the woman said. "What country you from?" she asked.

"*Country*?"

"You're killing me, honey. Come on."

"No! No, I won't hurt you!" I insisted, self-conscious now that Mama Luz must have marked me somehow.

The woman's eyes widened. "Uh, OK, princess, Why don't you just get comfy in there."

Princess? "You know me?" I asked, confused.

The woman narrowed her dark eyes at me and shook her head, equally confused. "If I knew you, I wouldn't have all these screens to fill out, now would I?"

I watched her hand gesture to the panel in front of her. "Screens…" I repeated, but this only made the woman's face pinch like she'd bitten into a pufferfish.

"Right… OK, sweetheart, do you know your name?"

"My name, yes! My name is Cora."

"And hallelujah, now we're getting somewhere. Is that Cora with a K or a C?"

I didn't know how to reply, afraid that whatever I might say would pinch her face again. "Just… Cora, of the sea."

"With a C, excellent," the woman said, poking again at the…*screen* in front of her.

"Do you know where I can find the captain?" I asked.

The woman laughed. "Yeah, he'll be here any minute now."

I was all at once nervous and excited at the prospect of seeing him again. I moved toward the humming bars in front of me without thinking, only to feel a current run through me when I got close. The bars crackled and flared until I took several steps backward.

"He will know me," I said, though I didn't know what I would say when I saw him…when he saw me, no longer as an Undine.

"Is that so?" the woman asked, then stopped poking at her screen. "Good, that will save us the trouble of shipping you to the Weigh Station," she finished.

"What's the…*Weigh Station*?"

"Where they determine if somebody dug that chip out of your neck or you never had one."

"Why?" I asked.

The woman blew out a long breath. "If you took out the chip, you go to Scrapper Island Penal Colony. If you never had one, the medics give you one," she finished, pointing to the place on her neck where gills would be if she were an Undine. She pointed to my neck, and I touched the still-burning sections of skin just below my ears. "Hey…" the woman said, her face pinching again. She got up from her seat and crossed to me, tilting her head to the side. "Swish those goldilocks back again, princess."

I looked at her, puzzled by the request, but I followed the motion of her hands and moved my hair off my shoulders.

"This is *swish*?"

"Yeah. That's swish. Why do you have two tamper marks instead of one? You go to some hack Grind medic who didn't know which side they put chips in?"

I shook my head, confused. "There are marks?" I asked, feeling the rough lines on either side of my throat.

"Why do I always get the hack jobs?" she asked, but it seemed she wasn't talking to me since she turned away and started poking at her screen again." So, what are those swirly tattoos you've got there?" she asked, this time, giving me a quick look. Even if I had known how to answer her, I didn't have the chance.

"Morning, Bev, anything interest—" a tall, silver-haired man dressed in black coverings like the woman came into the room, stopping in the middle of his sentence as he looked at me. His thick, black eyebrows crashed together. "And who's this?"

"Morning, Captain," the woman answered, but this was *not* the captain I'd seen. "Says her name is *Cora*. The Sweeper droids brought her in a little while ago without a census chip," the woman explained. "They picked her up by The Grind docks."

"He's not the captain I'm looking for. Is there another?" I said, startling both of them.

The man looked back over his shoulder at the woman. "Bev, what the hell is this about?"

"Your guess is as good as mine, sir. She said you'd know her."

"*Me*?"

"No! *Not* him. The *captain of the guard*," I clarified, but this only seemed to make *both* their faces pinch.

"She has tamper marks on both sides of her neck, sir."

"*Both* sides?" He turned to me. "Did you try to have your census chip taken out, Cora?"

I shook my head, still not knowing what that meant. The man raised both his dark eyebrows at me and ran a hand over his thinning silver hair as he looked more closely at where my gills used to be.

"Do you have another captain?" I asked, desperate to get out of this cage so I could find the captain and get this whole thing over with. The man took a deep breath and shook his head before blowing it out.

"Transfer her to the weigh station, Bev. Ericson can figure this one out," he said. "Call for a live patrol, but walk her to the car, and for God's sake, get her some more clothes."

Chapter 7

The woman named Bev gave me different coverings, a very tight, red covering she called a *tank top*, and loose, black leg coverings she called *sweatpants*. She also gave me an over covering called a *jacket* and coverings for my feet called *shoes*, but these made walking even more difficult because they were a little too big.

"Let's go, princess. The car won't wait all day," Bev said, waving for me to come through the flickering bars. "They're neutralized. Come on." I walked toward her, and she led me outside where a big, black box stretched out in front of us. She opened the side of it and motioned for me to get inside.

"Just the one?" a man *inside* the box said.

"Just her. Put her on the outgoing weigh station barge. Give a heads-up to Ericson. She's from *overseas*," Bev told the man.

"Ericson is back already? I thought he was on psych leave?"

"He passed the screening, I guess," Bev told him.

The man shrugged, then nodded to me. "OK. Hop in."

I looked at Bev, unsure of what the man meant. She motioned for me to move into the box. One of the cubes floated in next to me. It shot another small light at my wrists, making it impossible for me to move my arms.

"What—?" I started to ask, trying to keep my voice steady.

"Don't they have Sweepers in France...or wherever?" the man said, glancing back at me as an afterthought.

"Just move it. That barge leaves in thirty, and I don't want to keep her here until next week," Bev said.

The man nodded to her just before a black wall rose in front of me, blocking him from view. Bev closed the opening, and we started moving.

We were moving for some time before the sea came into view again. It looked just like the shoreline I'd seen earlier, but most of the small boats were gone. In their place, a large ship like the one Mama Luz had sunk rested against the docks. People were lined up, escorted by more *Sweepers*, as the man called them, and were one by one going aboard.

"This is your stop," he said as he opened the side of the box. The Sweeper moved first, making me follow because it hadn't released me from the light bonds.

We moved through the line of people until we made our way up to another man in black, this one wearing a black head covering and holding a panel that was made of lights. He held it up to each person, then poked at it like Bev had poked at her screen before motioning for each person to board the boat.

He held the panel up to me, then repositioned it and did it again.

He lowered it then and looked at my throat. "No chip?"

"Cens…Census?" I said, trying to remember what Bev and the captain had called it.

The man nodded. "That's right. Where's yours?"

I shook my head. He poked at the Sweeper and scanned his panel again. "All right. Weigh Station it is.

Section D2," he said, and the Sweeper led me onto the boat.

We walked past several people who looked very tired, some of them with bandages on their throats where gills would be if they were Undine. The Sweeper positioned me in front of one of the sectioned seats, each of them separated by a small raised half-wall on either side.

"Please sit and place your hands on your knees, palms down," the Sweeper said.

"Final call!" a dark-haired man said. He was facing away from me, but he was dressed in white rather than black like the other men.

"Who's that?" I asked the Sweeper.

"Please sit and place your hands on your knees, palms down," the Sweeper repeated.

I turned to sit where it directed me and tried to remember what knees were, but once seated, there was really only one place for my hands to go. As soon as my hands were in position, bars of light like the ones from the cage shot over them. I could feel the prickling they caused on my skin if I tried to raise them at all and started to panic a little. *What if I got an itch*? I thought. And of course, that was when it started.

I scrunched up my face desperate to make the feeling at the end of my nose stop, but it only seemed to make it worse. I turned into my shoulder to see if I could rub the itch out, but I couldn't *quite* reach the spot. I stuck out my bottom lip and tried to blow air upward as hard as I could, but all that did was cause a strand of my hair to fall into my face, the ends catching in the light bars. They crackled, and I panicked. I jerked forward, shocking my arms, which made me yell out.

"Sit back!" the man next to me shouted, but the shock didn't stop even when my arms moved away from the bars.

"I am! I am!"

"Turn it off!" a man yelled. Almost in the same breath the bars of light disappeared, though random shocks still came from nowhere. I bit my lip to keep from making any noise when I saw dark gashes, red and angry, crisscrossing over my forearms. "Be still—it's all right. Stop struggling. The jacket will stop the current, please." The man was suddenly in front of me, taking off his... *jacket* and wrapping it around my wounds. "Gibbons, finish the walkthrough and take us out if I'm not back."

"But, Captain—"

"Now! And send Peabody to sickbay."

"You're him. You're the...*captain*." I whispered to myself, but he heard me anyway.

"Yes, don't worry, we'll get this—" He looked up at me, his sea-blue eyes widening as his voice nearly disappeared. "*You...*"

I didn't know what to say, but I didn't have a chance to speak anyway when he blinked repeatedly and shook his head just before marshaling me below deck. I nearly tripped over my feet a few times because we were moving so quickly, but each time, he caught me around the waist and steadied me.

We went into a small area with shiny seats, one of them long and flat with a big, round light hanging above like a little sun. The pain in my arms was getting worse, but whenever I closed my eyes to brace against the pain, all I could see was my tail burning away and the two legs appearing.

"Captain? You sent for me?" A short, stout man rushed into the room out of breath, and his brown, thinning hair had been blown in all directions.

"Burns…." the captain started. He slowly unwrapped the jacket from my arms, and the pain intensified. I winced. "I'm sorry," he said. "This is Dr. Peabody. You'll be all right."

"The restraints again?" Dr. Peabody asked the captain.

"I'm going to rip them out of the seats myself if they don't get a qualified programmer in here once and for all," he said, not looking up from the jacket he was slowly trying to remove from my arms. I bit the inside of my cheek to keep from wincing again or even crying out, which was what I was all too close to doing.

"Let's have a look then," Dr. Peabody said, waving his hands under a blue light against the wall, then moving toward me with his hands extended. He took my wrists and laid my palms over my knees, and I saw my hands shaking from the pain.

"Don't you have anything to numb it?" the captain asked, his jaw tight and his dark eyebrows drawn together.

"Just give me a second." Dr. Peabody raised one hand, which contained a small, white cube with a blue line running down the side. He pressed the top of it and a mist fell over the burns on my arms, cooling them until I didn't feel any pain at all. I let out a big breath, which came out ragged.

The captain took several steps backward while Dr. Peabody applied another spray which turned blue and puffed into a thin foam over each burn. He wound a white wrap around my forearms and I was suddenly, uncontrollably tired.

"What's wrong with her?" the captain asked.

"The anesthesia is just hitting her bloodstream," the doctor answered, then met my eyes. "You'll sleep right through the repair, don't worry."

"Repair?" I managed to ask, my voice feeling like it was floating away from me.

"Good as new in the morning when we make landfall. Help her to the bunk, Nicholas? Careful with the wraps. They're still curing."

The captain—*Nicholas?*—moved toward me, but I couldn't keep him in focus as my vision blurred and it got harder and harder to keep my eyes open. His arm moved around my waist, and I fell against him when he helped me down, my feet feeling like they were just melting into the floor.

"Whoa…whoa," I heard him say just before the room was swallowed in a whirlpool of black. "How are you here?" he whispered, his other arm moving under my legs and lifting me off the ground. I thought he was talking to me, but it was soon clear he was talking to himself. "It's not her, fool. They don't exist. They don't exist…" he trailed off.

It really was him. He really did remember me, even if he didn't seem to believe it. I was overcome with joy and warmth and compassion for all he'd been through when the Lawless Undine had attacked his ship until, like a rogue wave crashing down on me, I remembered that I was here to kill him.

Chapter 8

The room was empty when I opened my eyes, but my arms didn't hurt anymore. I tried to pull the hard, blue shell covering from them, but they seemed stuck. I sat up and tried to stand, distrustful of these legs that had failed me earlier.

I found the shoes Bev had given me and slipped them on, scrunching up to the front of the shoe so they wouldn't fall off. My head spun a little as I started walking, so I stayed as close to the wall as I could until I made my way out of the room.

The boat was still, which seemed strange. Had we already arrived at the Weigh Station?

I started to climb the stairs leading to the upper deck, then thought better of it. What if they sent me to the island Bev mentioned, or to the medic to give me a census chip? Either of those places would take me away from the captain, and I couldn't allow that. I might never find him again, and then Reed would die. *I* would die… I needed to focus. I needed to remember that killing the captain was a strategical act.

Humans had been selfish since the beginning, hadn't they? Just consuming and destroying everything throughout the centuries? Maybe Mara was right. The Undine had hidden long enough. We'd run long enough. But none of this made figuring out how to make the captain kiss me any easier. *He* had to kiss *me*, Mama Luz had specified. I couldn't even ambush him!

People talking above startled me out of my thoughts, and the creak of their approaching steps down the stairs made me scramble to return to the other side of the room. I bolted from where I stood, but my legs were not accustomed to turning over so quickly and I fell face-first onto the hard, wooden planks below.

The footsteps began clamoring down the stairs and soon, the voices filled the room.

"My dear, my dear!" Dr. Peabody said, rushing to my side. "You shouldn't be out of bed. Help me, Nicholas."

A strong arm moved under my shoulders and lifted me from the floor. It was the captain, who looked at me warily this time before he looked away. He carried me stiffly back to the...*bed*, as Dr. Peabody called it, and nearly dropped me into it before putting space between us.

Dr. Peabody moved closer and sat on the edge of the bed. "Just hold still for a minute, please," he said as he waved a small, colorful screen over my head, and it finally occurred to me that a *minute* must be a small bit of time...a few breaths. "The anesthesia is still in her system, but it should be clear in about ten minutes," he said. *Twenty breaths, thirty...?* I thought. "She can be moved with assistance."

"Will she be able to stand on her own for the medic's evaluation?" the captain asked without looking at me. He stood tall and straight, clasping his hands in front of him.

Dr. Peabody held one finger in front of my face and moved it from side to side. "How do you feel, my dear? Dizzy?"

"Dizzy?" I asked. Dr. Peabody just nodded.

"She may need *fifteen* minutes, but perhaps the open air will clear her head. Show me your arms dear," he said, glancing down at the blue shell coverings. I held them out to him, and he raised a small, silver cube that made a high-pitched, deafening sound. My hands flew to my ears and I nearly fell to the floor until the sound abruptly stopped.

"What was that!? What did you do?" the captain asked.

Dr. Peabody shook his head. "Not a thing! Just turned on the ultrasonic to remove the derma casing on her burns. Are you all right, my dear?"

I nodded and lowered my hands. He held out his for my arms, and when I hesitated, he set the small, silver cube down on the ground. He smiled a little and started to break away the shell casing over my arms, and I was astonished to see the dark gashes, and even the bite wound I'd had, were nearly gone.

"They're healed…" I said under my breath.

"Yes, dear, just about! When you're ready, then, Nicholas, just help her get above for some air. I need to queue the others for the medics."

The captain nodded as Dr. Peabody patted my hand and left the small room. I hadn't noticed all the shiny objects hanging on the walls all around, some of them sharp, some of them like bubbles, clear and rounded filled with tufts of something white.

"Who are you?" the captain asked abruptly.

"I'm…" I started, but I couldn't tell him who I really was. Bev and the other captain hadn't understood, and I had the feeling telling him I'd come from the sea to kill him *probably* wouldn't go over well.

"Your file says your name is Cora, and you're from *overseas*," he said.

"Yes," was all I could think to say.

"You don't really understand me, do you?" I just looked at him and nodded, which seemed to be neutral enough. He blew out a breath and seemed to relax his stiff posture. "Sorry, you just look like someone I'm not even sure I really saw," he added, shaking his head. "I know that doesn't make sense. You couldn't be her, anyway…" He took in a deep breath and looked at me more kindly this time. "Do you think you can stand?"

I nodded again and put my feet on the floor, making sure I was steady before I tried to rise this time. I got up slowly as the captain took a few steps toward me, his arm held out to me. I took it, and he escorted me to the stairs.

The boat was docked when we got to the top of the stairs. In the distance was a small island with dense trees and a long, white shelter stretching back from the shore. Next to us, two other boats, these long and narrow, were bobbing in the current.

A line of people wound toward the white shelter waiting for their turn to go inside as another line wound back onto the boat. Both lines were patrolled by Sweepers.

"This is the…Wave Station?" I asked.

The captains lips quirked." *Weigh* Station, yes. Do you want to tell me how you got those marks on your throat?" He glanced quickly at me and tightened my arm in his, but it seemed more tactical than endearing. I would have done the same if I were afraid someone was about to dart away from custody.

"I have no...*chip*," I said.

"Not *now*, anyway." He almost smiled. "What happened to your throat, Cora?"

"I..." I started, and then realized there was no possible way I could tell him.

He nodded and loosened his hold on my arm as we approached the opening to the Weigh Station.

"You're next. Are you still dizzy?" he asked, letting go of my arm. I nodded and stepped into one of the lines inside.

Several people in long, white jackets held small, silver devices against the throats of the people coming to them. Most of those being examined went directly into light bonds and were escorted out another door by the Sweepers.

I turned to the captain. "Where are they taking them?"

"Back onto the boat—we'll drop them off at Scrapper Island Penal Colony before going back to the mainland with anyone who never had a chip to begin with."

"What happens to them?"

"After they get a chip here, they'll go into the system. The Citadel says they try to find jobs for them, but it's easier to let them slip into debt and collect their years— one less person taking up oxygen."

There was so much I didn't understand from what he'd said, so I just shook my head at him and asked about the one word I could remember. "*Citadel*?"

"Sorry, sorry... I shouldn't have said that." He smiled awkwardly and glanced at the floor. "The Citadel is a protected city where all the decisions are made. Don't worry—I'll make sure your job placement doesn't slip through the cracks."

"Name?" an older woman with short, dark hair asked. She wore a long white coat like the others receiving people from a line. I hadn't even realized I'd moved up so many spaces.

"Cora. My name is Cora," I answered.

"Cora what?"

"Yes, Cora."

The woman pressed her lips into a thin line and tilted her head at me. "OK, *Cora*, where did the marks on your throat come from?" She held the little silver device under each of my ears.

I struggled for a reply until I remembered that the captain had told Dr. Peabody I had *burns* on my arms, and those had felt the same as whatever Mama Luz had done to my gills. The marks everyone had mentioned must have looked similar.

"They're burns," I finally answered.

The woman raised a thin, dark eyebrow. "Burns from what?"

"Um…a… powder."

The woman's dark eyes widened at this. She pushed her bottom lip out and nodded absently to me as she moved the small, silver device back and forth over the marks that were apparently on my throat. Suddenly, her expression shifted to one of confusion.

"Sandra, can I borrow your imager for a second? Mine's… off."

The woman receiving the line next to us handed over her little silver device, and I was scanned again.

"What's the problem?" the captain asked.

"She has two sets of vocal cords, and her respiratory anatomy doesn't seem entirely...*right*."

"What does that mean?" the captain asked quickly. "No chip then? Never had one?"

"Uh, no. No, I don't see any extraction scars on the tendons," the woman answered, meeting my eyes. "Step over to the table please. I'll be right over." She smiled absently and walked toward a group of others in long, white coats who were actively poking at screens on the other side of the room.

The captain took my arm tightly as he had before and started steering me toward the opening where the other line was exiting.

"She said to go to the...*table*," I said, struggling to remember the word.

"No, something's wrong. You lie down on that table, and you won't get back up," he said in a quiet, steady voice. "We're getting out of here."

Chapter 9

We moved quickly into the line heading back toward the ship, and the captain stood between me and the Sweepers until we got to the beach. But instead of going back onto his ship, we turned toward one of the long, white boats docked next to it.

"Get in and stay low," he said, letting my arm go and helping me over the nose of the boat into the front seat. He looked around, then got in on the other side and poked at the screens that stretched the width of the boat. "*Damnit,*" he growled, but then put both hands on the wheel and spoke again. "Commandeer code 119. Captain Nicholas Ericson. Weigh Station, Bermuda Two."

The boat roared to life, and the screens in front of us all lit up at once.

"What did you do?" I asked, noticing a few of the people who were still in line turning to look at us as we pulled away from the shore and sped toward the horizon.

"I just called for security crews—only way to start the boat. Hopefully, they'll be too busy finding out there is absolutely *nothing* wrong here to come after us right away." He grinned.

"Wh—Where are we going?" I asked, but the deafening sound of the motor replaced any chance of an answer.

The land slipped farther into the distance until I couldn't see it at all on the horizon behind us anymore, only the whitecap wake of the boat. For some time there was nothing but ocean in any direction, and I had no idea whatsoever where we were in relation to the Southern Depths, let alone home.

***

It seemed like half the day had passed before we stopped at a small, overgrown beach, and my face felt too tightly stretched when I tried to talk again.

"Where are we?"

"A dead zone," the captain answered, stepping into the water, then, carefully through the dense vegetation. "They shouldn't be able to track us here, at least not for a few days," he added as he moved to a nearby tree and started shaking it.

I stared at him. "*What* are you doing?"

"Trying to drop these coconuts," he answered, then took out a small blade that looked a lot like my short spear. I cursed at myself for not taking it with me when Mama Luz sent me ashore. "OK, stand back," he said, then put the blade between his teeth and started climbing the trunk.

Two brown, *hairy* fruits fell to the ground as he finished cutting them from the top of the tree. One rolled over my feet, and I was surprised to find it hard as a rock when I picked it up.

The captain made his way down the tree, slipping on the last step and falling on his back. His blade went sailing into the brush.

"Are you all right?" I asked.

He groaned, but rolled over and pushed up to his feet. "Fine," he said, scowling as he searched the ground.

I bent down and picked up his blade, which was sticking straight out of the sand not far from me. "Lucky that knife didn't land in your foot," he said, extending his hand for it.

"*Knife...*" I said under my breath and handed it to him. He motioned for me to hand him the hairy fruit as well.

"What is this?" I asked.

He raised a dark eyebrow at me. "This? You've never seen a *coconut*?"

I shrugged. "They don't grow where I'm from." As soon as the words left my lips, I wished I could unsay them. I turned away from him, hoping he wouldn't ask me where, exactly, that was. But I wasn't that lucky.

"Your file said you were picked up by Sweeper Droids just beyond the docks in The Grind."

"The what?"

"Sorry, the city outside The Citadel." I watched his mouth form the words, his dark brows dance with expression as he poked the tip of his knife into different parts of the brown fruit. "And *The Citadel* is where the Sweepers took you *after* they picked you up," he finished, then folded his legs under him and put the coconut on the ground. He drove the tip of his knife into it, then picked up a nearby rock and hit the handle several times. He did this repeatedly until the blade sunk through the brown shell. He pulled it out and handed me the coconut. "Here, drink it."

I took it and raised it to my mouth, which was so dry, I didn't even care about the strange aftertaste of the water inside.

"Thank you," I said, handing it back to him. He took a long drink, then raised the coconut over his head and brought it down over the rock he'd just used. It cracked open, and I was surprised to see that the inside was stark white.

"This is the meat," he said, scraping chunks of it out with his knife and handing me one of the halves.

"Meat from *fruit*?" I asked.

He just smiled at me. "Eat it—it's good. And you'll need your strength. We have a long walk ahead of us."

"Where are we going?"

"First, you tell me how you came to be on the beach at The Grind docks," he said, putting a pinch of the coconut meat into his mouth.

"I…I don't remember," I lied, but what else could I say? *A Gnome rowed me there through a mystical fog that magically cut the distance in half so I could find you and kill you?*

I put the coconut meat into my mouth and was surprised to find that it was sweet.

The captain laughed quietly. "You like it."

"I didn't expect it to be sweet."

"No, I guess the water wasn't," he said, glancing up at me, his smile fading. "And the hard shell on the outside was misleading, don't you think?" He glanced at me again, this time meeting my eyes. "It seems like something completely different from what it really is."

I took another bite of the coconut meat and looked through the overhanging vegetation out onto the sea.

"You left your men. Won't you be imprisoned?"

He laughed. "Doubtful. They'll just assume they were right about me coming back too early and will give me a desk job. I've probably lost my ship, though."

I felt him watching me, waiting for me to ask him. Waiting for me to show that I already knew what he'd gone through.

I didn't trust myself to look at him yet, so again, I asked the tide. "Were you traveling?"

He laughed again, this time, less abruptly. "Something like that."

I risked a glance at him. "Was it like this place? Was it beautiful where you were?"

He found my eyes, and a hint of a smile crossed his lips. "A part of it was."

So this was the game we were playing then. Both of us evading the other's question, or answering others that were never asked. It took everything in my power to keep my expression neutral. I wanted to tell him who I really was, where I really came from. I wanted to ask for his help as a fellow soldier in strategizing a way out of the situation I was in, but that would only mean Mama Luz would surely kill Reed…*and me.*

"It's like time stands still here," I said before I could say anything I would regret.

"I said the same thing the first time I was here," he said, pushing his dark hair back from his eyes. "The ship that was attacked wasn't the first I'd lost. We were caught in a storm once, years ago… We managed to stay upright, but it was impossible to stay on course. Punched a hole in the hull somehow, and we wound up stuck here for a week waiting for The Citadel to pick up our distress call."

The hairs on my arms stood on end at the thought that there could be Lawless Undine here. That they would do something to the boat we'd just hidden.

I scanned the water for any sign of them, but of course, I saw nothing.

"You were lucky," I said, hearing the note of warning in my voice.

"That's what they keep telling me." He nodded to the ground as he pulled in a deep breath and got to his feet. "We should get moving. It's a long way to where we're going."

"Where *are* we going?"

"To see an old friend of mine. I need to cash in a favor."

***

We walked until the sun was low in the sky, and I continued to worry about the Lawless Undine sabotaging our boat. There would be nothing I could do to protect the captain without my short spear or my Undine voice. I would just sound like all the humans sounded to us, and who knew if these Lawless would even understand that.

Wait, protect him? I thought. All so I could kill him myself.

I shook away the thought because the idiocy of it was too distracting. I needed to get him to kiss me somehow, and what better place to do that than here, close to the sea? I had no idea where we were above the skim, but underwater, I was sure I'd be able to find my way back to the outskirts of The Shallows, where Mama Luz's boat would be waiting with Reed for two more days.

"So, your friend… What's the favor you're going to call in?" I asked as we made our way through the thinning vegetation. We must have been approaching the edge of a town.

The captain looked over his shoulder in answer. "We're going to need some supplies. Probably another boat."

"Another boat?" I startled at this. Was he worried about ours being attacked too?

He gave me a curious look, his clear blue eyes narrowing under his dark, furrowed brow. "Yeah. The Citadel will be able to find this one after a few days. This place is in a dead zone, but that's just for the average scanners. When they don't pick us up on those, they'll bring out the others to increase the reach."

I exhaled in relief, though in a few days, none of that would matter. Either he would be dead, or I would.

"What's your friend's name?" I asked, trying to change the subject and escape the looming dread it brought me.

"Dr. Zee," he said. "We're almost there."

The bite wound on my arm was starting to itch and redden again, which I didn't understand because it had been almost gone after the treatment on the boat. *Maybe I should have waited for the saline treatment from the healer like Reed insisted,* I thought, but there was only going forward now. If there was an issue, this Dr. Zee would likely notice and treat it.

But again, none of it would matter in two days.

Chapter 10

When the brush and overgrown vegetation finally cleared, we came upon a small shelter made from the materials all around. It was all tree trunks and mud, with a roof made of thatching. The captain knocked on the weathered screen door.

"You mus' be from elsewhere if you're knocking," an older man's voice said in an accent like the sailors who always come from the Southern Depths. "Come on, then."

The door creaked when the captain pushed it open, and around the corner sat an older man with very tanned skin, his white hair and brows a stark contrast to his dark eyes. He was thin and wore an embroidered blue shirt with ornate designs running vertically down each side.

"Dr. Zee…" the captain said, making the old man's face light in a wide, almost toothless smile.

"*Que milagro*, look at this son of Eve come back to me," he said, which nearly stopped my heart. *Son of Eve*? That was what Mama Luz called the captain. "And who…?' The man trailed off when he met my eyes, his wide smile falling just a little. "Who is this pretty *señorita*?"

"Doctor, this is Cora."

"*Cora* is it?" Dr. Zee's lips flinched and his dark eyes widened as he looked into me more than at me. "What a beautiful name…"

He extended his hand to me for some reason, the skin on his arms thin and fragile, like a spiderweb weighed down with dew in the morning. He made my own skin prickle.

"Ah, she's from…overseas," the captain said, as if in apology.

Dr. Zee nodded and smiled widely again. "Undine…"

My heart started pounding so loudly, I was sure both men would hear it too. "*What did you say?*"

"I said, *indeed*," he answered, giving me a closed lip smile. "May I?" He glanced down at my arm and held out his hand.

"That should have been healed by now," the captain said, puzzled when he saw the bite wound. "The restraints on my ship malfunctioned and burned her."

"This is no burn, *muchacho*." The doctor cradled my forearm and led me over to a small area that looked like a makeshift infirmary. Several differently-colored and shaped bottles with corks in them lined the shelves, which hung over several folded pieces of cloth and a few strange instruments. He picked up one of these, a lens bound in a thin wooden frame, and held it over the bite wound on my arm.

"Who bit you, Cora?" the doctor asked.

"Ah…bit me? No…nothing bit me," I lied as it occurred to me there was no way for me to explain how I'd been bitten to the captain.

Dr. Zee fixed his dark eyes on mine, one white brow arching. "Not *what*, child. *Who*?"

"And *when*?" the captain asked, taking a step toward us. "She's been in my care since the seat restraints malfunctioned. If she already had a bite wound, it would have been healed by the derma packs my ship surgeon used on her."

"Not this sort of bite, *muchacho*." Dr. Zee looked more closely at my arm.

The captain met my eyes. "He said, *who*…Cora, a *person* bit you?"

"I… I don't know," I stammered. Why couldn't I think of *something* to say? "Maybe, a small shark?"

"You were in the water?" The captain's dark brows crashed over his narrowed eyes. "When? Before the Sweepers picked you up near the docks?"

"Ah…I—I'm not sure," I stammered again, realizing I'd only made everything ten times *harder*. I needed to stop talking.

The doctor looked at the captain for a long time before he nodded and gave me another closed-lip smile.

"Let's see what can be done for this, aye?" he said with a small nod. He took down one of the brown jars from the shelf and dripped some of its muddy contents onto a tuft of white…*sponge*? He squeezed it over the bite wound, and it started burning worse than when I'd been bitten in the first place. I sucked in a quick breath and pressed my lips together, afraid that if I didn't, I would scream.

"What is that?" the captain asked.

"Iron, mostly. Some copper, zinc…" Dr. Zee looked at me like I should've had a reaction to this, but the only reaction I was having was *pain*.

"It *burns*," I said through my teeth, but then the pain became maddening and I ran to the faucet near the back of the room to wash off the concoction.

The burning on the surface subsided, but the searing pain seemed to sink into the muscles in my arm…into the bones, finally spreading down to my fingers and up into my shoulder.

"Are you all right?" the captain asked, moving to my side.

"It hurts…inside my arm now. It's getting worse."

"Just doing its job," Dr. Zee said, crossing to us and pouring a warm liquid over the wound, which completely neutralized the pain. The bite mark was no longer red or swollen. In fact, it was almost unnoticeable, save for the semicircle of broken skin. Dr. Zee rubbed something that looked like clay over this, then started washing his hands.

"Let that dry until it cracks. It'll fall off when it's done doin' what it does," he said without looking up at me. He shook his hands dry and showed us back to the front room, stopping to grab a bag. "Now, follow me to the market and tell me why you come all this way to see old Dr. Zee."

***

The market was alive with people talking, trading and trying not to run into each other. Dr. Zee didn't approach any of the wide baskets of multi-colored fruits and vegetables that were almost too intriguing to resist. I'd never seen them up close like this with the fruit on the island in The Shallows being so far up the beach.

"Those are called mangoes," Dr. Zee said just off my shoulder, startling me. "*Dos, por favor,*" he said to the woman behind the spread of yellow fruits that were kissed red in places by the sun.

"Mangoes..." I repeated when he handed one of them to me. I held it up to my nose and breathed in the sweet, rich scent.

Dr. Zee smiled. "Don't have these where you're from, eh?" he asked, not apparently interested in the answer as he turned and kept walking. The captain pulled out a small blade from his pocket and took the fruit from my hand.

He sliced the fruit down the center and handed half to me. He raised his half to his mouth and scraped his teeth along the inside peel. I did the same, but was surprised by the deluge of liquid that escaped. The captain laughed as he swallowed the last of his mango and brushed away the fruit water from my cheek with his hand.

A smile settled on his face." Juicy..." he almost laughed." When they're soft on the outside like this, that's how you know they're ripe."

I flinched at the word, remembering the crew aboard his ship who tried to attack Opal and me. The captain's smile fell away in the same moment a small, black creature snatched the rest of the mango from my hand and scurried up a nearby tree to eat it. "What is that?" I asked breathlessly, my heart hammering in my chest.

The captain laughed again. "That is a hungry little monkey," he said, tossing the rest of his mango to it. "No monkeys where you're from either, then..." he stated instead of asked, studying me when I looked back to him. I hurried to catch up to Dr. Zee before he could ask me anything else.

"My mother took me to this market when I was a child. Same with her mother, and her mother's mother, since the market first came to be," he said, his gaze traveling over all the goods, all the people.

"How long ago was that?"

"Maybe a month or so after the beginning of time." Dr. Zee turned to look at me intently. His hard expression softened after another few seconds, and his smile turned into a hearty laugh. The captain made his way to my other side, and the doctor composed himself as we made our way out of the market and back onto the earthen path that brought us here. "So, what brings you to Snake Island, then?"

"We need your help, Dr. Zee. A place to rest tonight, a boat and some supplies for tomorrow."

"A boat? Did you risk a swim here, *mi hijo*?"

The captain smiled. "The boat we brought here can be traced after a few days. I'll need to smash the batteries in it, if you can help us with a replacement."

"Somebody in pursuit of you then?"

"It's a long story, but mainly, we left before something could be done to Cora."

"I see." Dr. Zee nodded to the path in front of us. Small blue and red flowers interwoven on vines that seemed to lace the entire dense, green path. "You're always welcome *en mi casa*, of course. And I have a fishing boat that's twice as old as you, but you're welcome to see if you can bring her back to life. She's in the marina."

"Thank you." The captain exhaled like the weight of the entire sea had just been lifted from him.

We turned the corner and came upon the doctor's home again, where he dropped the bag of goods inside and took us around the back.

"Hello, *bonita*," the doctor said to a box, this one sea green and more rounded than the black one that had taken me to the captain's ship. "This car may be older than the boat." He laughed.

"*Car…*" I repeated to myself, then caught the captain watching me.

"Get in," the doctor said. The captain opened the side of the car and motioned for me to go in first. He sat next to me, and the doctor pulled a small, shiny stick from his shirt and pushed it into a slot. The car roared and started to shake.

"Her bark is worse than her bite," the doctor said.

The captain shook his head, amazed. "This must be at least a hundred years old."

The doctor nodded. "*Bonita* likes the old tropics life."

We moved along the earthen path slowly, but more quickly than if we were walking. It wound over a rise that overlooked the sea, which seemed so quiet and peaceful from this distance. I wondered how Reed was, if Opal had made it safely back to my mother and the Guard. And I wondered how I would ever manage to kill the man who had saved me not once, but twice.

Chapter 11

"Likely needs airing out below," the doctor said. "She's been in that slip awhile."

"Are there tools aboard?" the captain asked.

The doctor shrugged." Maybe in the engine room. Climb aboard and let me know what you need. I can bring it back from the house."

The captain nodded and climbed aboard the boat, leaving me with Dr. Zee standing outside of the car.

"Were you a fisherman?" I asked as the captain disappeared below deck.

"Of sorts," he said, nodding, but he didn't look at me. "How did you come to meet the good captain?"

I started over two or three times in my mind trying to figure out how to answer him. I couldn't tell him the truth, and I couldn't even tell him the *half*-truth about the leaving the Weigh Station before they could find out why I was different.

I finally just repeated what the captain had said earlier. "It's…a long story."

"You got yourself into some trouble?" he asked, glancing at the marks on my neck. "Some…*deep* trouble?"

I suddenly felt insecure and moved my hand over the marks, but they felt different. There were only two raised lines instead of the three. I touched the other side of my throat and felt the same thing—only two instead of three.

"No visible issues!" the captain shouted from the deck, startling me. "I'm going to start her up."

The doctor nodded to the captain, who disappeared again below deck, and my heart started pounding in my chest. *Two lines…two days…there were only two days left now.*

"That's a good man up there," Dr. Zee said, again without looking at me.

I glanced at him. "I know."

"Not all of them are."

The doctor's voice became steadier, fuller when he said this, and for an instant it felt like the ground moved under my feet—a tremor so short I wondered if it happened at all.

"Did you feel that?" I asked.

The boat growled to life, spitting and coughing at first, but then the engine started to regulate. We heard the captain's muted celebratory cheers from below deck.

The doctor laughed. "Good man…" He glanced at me, his dark eyes flitting again to my throat before he started clapping his hands and walking toward the boat to meet the captain, who had just come out to the railing.

I was frozen where I stood. Why did everything he just said feel like…a warning?

"It works!" the captain shouted to me, pulling me back from my thoughts.

"We'll celebrate tonight," Dr. Zee called up to him. "The sun will be going down soon. But there should be some fly rods below. Take her around the island and catch us a feast, *muchacho*. I'll come back in a bit with supplies."

The doctor looked at me longer than was comfortable before he went back to his box—er, his…*car*—and disappeared back down the path. I followed the captain's gestures and climbed onto the ship to meet him.

"You ever been fishing, Cora?" he asked as he disappeared again below deck. He emerged a few seconds later with two long poles. He walked me to the far side of the boat and leaned over the railing.

"No, I haven't…not with a rod, anyway." The captain looked at me, surprised.

"Nets?"

I nodded, realizing it would be the closest thing he could understand to skimming for krill or even small fish.

"What's that?" I asked, nodding to the bait tied to the end of the line. It looked alive, but it wasn't.

"It's a fly lure. I'll show you how it works, but we need to get on the outside of the shoreline first," he said, setting down the rods and moving into the small covered room that led below deck. I scanned the horizon feeling like we were being watched, but the water was calm.

Maybe too calm.

The boat moved slowly out of dock, and the shoreline soon fell away. In what seemed like no time at all we came around to the side of the island where we first landed. The boat we'd left under the overgrown vegetation seemed untouched.

"Captain?" I called to him. The engine of the boat downshifted and we stopped moving.

"Call me *Nicholas*," he said with a smile, startling me with how quickly and quietly he appeared at my side.

"I was going to ask if we should—" I started, but stopped when he pulled his shirt over his head. His shoulders and back were broad and muscular, but also dotted with various scars. A few small and round, and others long and thin. He turned to me and I gasped before I could stop myself. His chest was shadowed in dark hair that followed a line down the center of his sectioned abdomen. Most of the male Undine were lean like he was, but their torsos were plated with smooth, armored scales.

"What's wrong?" he asked, his heavy eyebrows arching.

"Ah…nothing. I just didn't expect to see…*you*." I stammered like a halfling.

"Oh." The captain's—*Nicholas's*—smile returned, and his clear blue eyes disappeared under the sweep of his thick, black lashes when he looked at the deck. A wash of color kissed his cheeks as his smile turned to a mischievous grin. "Well, I didn't pack for the trip, so I'm afraid I'll have to startle you one more time," he added, dropping his pants and jumping over the railing in nothing more than a dark blue covering that seemed like half pants, only much tighter than the white uniform pants he had been wearing.

He dove into the water and swam below the skim most of the way to the boat we brought here. When he finally surfaced next to the nose of the boat, he opened a panel near the front and began tugging at something. I watched his long arms reach, the muscles flexing and contracting until finally, he pulled out a rectangular black box and carried it to the rock he'd used to break open the coconut when we first arrived. There, he smashed it and took a small, silver piece from the wreckage only to smash that, too, against the rock with a nearby coconut shell.

He tossed the coconut shell aside and with a dusting of his hands, waded into the water and swam back. He moved like he'd been born an Undine, his long, smooth strokes propelling him back to this boat as quickly as I could imagine any of my kind. I turned away from him as he pulled himself onto the deck because I didn't want him to see me watching him, but it was almost impossible to look anywhere but at him.

He met my eyes and fought the grin pulling at the corners of his mouth. I forced myself to look away, to look back at the overgrown forest in front of us... anywhere but at the play of muscles alongside his hips as he approached.

I cleared my throat. "That must have been the device the people back from the Weigh Station would be able to track?" I asked, even though I already knew the answer.

"Not them, the ones from The Citadel, but yes," he said, the smile evident in his voice... He *knew* I was trying not to watch him, even now, and the certainty of this made me fight the smile threatening to break free across my own lips.

My lips... I thought, and all levity faded away. My lips would kill this man. I needed to remember this. I needed to stop letting myself get distracted.

"Are you all right?" he asked.

I pulled in a deep breath, which still ached a little to do. "Yes, thank you. Just a little anxious about someone taking us away from this place," I said, which wasn't entirely untrue.

"I won't let that happen." He stood next to me for another few seconds, then bent to catch my eyes. "I promise."

I smiled at him. "Nicholas… Why did you help me? Not just on your ship, but at the Weigh Station. You even stayed in line with me."

He let his eyes fall to the sea underneath us. "I suppose I wanted more time," he finally said, then seemed to be searching for something in my expression. "More time just to be sure."

"Of what?"

"Well, that's the funny part." He laughed. "When you asked me earlier if I had been traveling when I was gone… My ship was attacked a few days before. My whole crew, lost, except for me."

"I'm so sorry," I said, not as a general gesture the way someone might, but because I felt responsible even though I'd tried to stop the Lawless from attacking.

He leaned on the railing, dripping as he gazed out again on the water. "The Citadel thought I was in shock when I told them what really happened. When I stuck to my story, they wanted to send me to some psychiatric hospital," he added, laughing again and shaking his head. "I wasn't about to do that, so I told them what they wanted to hear."

"What did you tell them?" I asked.

"That some of the men fell asleep on their watch, and a prisoner set off a bomb in the stockade transport below deck. The boat sank, and then the sharks came."

"No, I mean about what *really* happened. What was it they wouldn't believe?"

He looked up me, studying me as if to gauge if he could trust me.

No…to gauge if I would believe him.

"There are stories sailors tell. I've been Captain of the Guard for eight years. Been a sailor since I was sixteen. I always just thought they were stories until I saw them with my own eyes."

"What did you see?" I asked, holding his guarded gaze.

"Mermaids," he finally said with the last of a breath. "But they weren't like the storybooks, or even the sailor stories. They were…*vicious*." He pulled in a deep breath and blew it out over the sea. "My men were stupid," he said, shaking his head again. "It's like they were possessed or something, actually climbing over each other to get down to the water. And when they did…" He trailed off. "Well, they just didn't come back."

"I'm so sorry," I repeated, wishing I could find a way to reverse the whole thing.

"Two of the mermaids seemed to be caught in the crossfire of it all. A child—if that's what you even call it—and an older one, my age, it seemed. That one looked at me like she would only kill me if I hurt the child." He spoke absently to the water, lost in memory.

"How could you tell?" I risked asking.

"It was a look in her eyes," he answered. "I've only ever seen it in other soldiers. It was a look that said she would die before she'd surrender." He turned to me then, his eyes fixed on mine, but softer. Searching. "I guess I helped you at the Weigh Station because I saw the same look in your eyes when the medic told you that you weren't like the others—when it seemed she would take you away."

"I didn't want to go to the prison island," I said too quickly.

"And your tattoos," he added, moving his hands lightly over my shoulders." She had some that were similar, right here, in the same place you do."

He leaned in, his black hair dripping over his chest as he raised his hand to my cheek. I felt his other hand slide around to the small of my back and pull me closer. His thumb moved over my bottom lip, and all at once it was like a bolt of lightning flashed in my mind. The feeling of Mama Luz's fingers pressing the white powder over my mouth...I felt it all over again—saw her all over again sprinkle the jar of it into the sea.

I pulled away abruptly, confused. I'd ruined the chance to save Reed, to go home, and who knew if there would be another opportunity now before my time was up?

"I'm...so sorry." Nicholas pushed his hands through his dark hair and reached for his white shirt, which stuck to his wet skin when he put it on.

"No, don't be. I'm sorry," I stammered, unsure of what to say next until I saw a fluttering in the water several lengths out. "That startled me," I lied. "Do you see that?"

But even more intriguing was the sound of singing Undine just beneath the skim. It started like a breeze through the dense foliage, wispy and blended until it evolved into a stronger, deeper, thrum. They were *hunting*.

"I do see it," Nicholas whispered as he reached for the fishing rod. "When it's agitated like that, it's called *nervous water*. There's a school of bonefish feeding right there," he added, checking the fly at the end of the line, then cocking an eyebrow at me. "Let's give them what they want."

Everything inside me wanted to pull the rod from his hands and throw it across the deck, but I wasn't afraid for the Undine that I knew were below. I was afraid for him —*for us*—and it was the realization that I was now aligned with him instead of the Undine that paralyzed me.

He held the rod high over our heads and whipped it forward. The fly sailed far into the distance and landed in the center of the agitation—in the center of the unsuspecting fray that I knew would vanish as quickly as it had appeared not because the fish had been feeding, but because they had been surrounded and driven into the shallow waters. There, the Undine hid in the refractions of light, closing around the fish until there was nowhere left for them to go. A few seconds later, it was over.

"Why do you call it *nervous* water?" I asked when the agitation abruptly stopped. "Why do you call it a *feeling*?"

Nicholas pulled in his line with an audible sigh of disappointment. "I haven't really thought about it before," he said, casting the line again. "I suppose part of it just looks like it's trembling from up here. Like it's afraid." He laughed. "I don't know. It's an expression."

I nodded, watching the skim for flashes of silver or slices of smooth, glassy black, but I didn't see or hear another trace of the Undine.

"It is afraid," I whispered to myself. "And it should be."

Chapter 12

I wrestled with my thoughts the whole way back to the marina.

We were far from Mama Luz's barge, I was sure. The Undine I'd just heard couldn't have been from Mara's clan, nor could they have known about the Gnome Queen's demands of me. They *must* have known the boat was occupied when the fly hit the water, but they didn't attack.

They didn't attack, I thought. And maybe that meant Mama Luz's pending war with the humans wasn't as widely spread as Mara had made it seem.

Nicholas had caught four large bonefish by the time we returned to the marina, where Dr. Zee was ashore waiting for us in the thinning grass with a large crate and a bag.

"Anything biting out there?" he called to us. Nicholas held the string of fish out the window, the engine sputtering as it turned off. Dr. Zee beamed at us as he lit the wood he'd apparently built up while he waited for us to return to shore.

"Look at all this! I didn't realize we were gone that long," Nicholas said as we approached. He nodded to the crate and the fire.

"I may be old," Dr. Zee chuckled. "But I'm efficient."

"Thank you for helping us," I said, noticing that the items in the crate were different instruments, but not like the ones I'd seen back in the infirmary—these looked like they were used to fix machines, not people. The bag was also nearly spilling over with colorful vegetables.

"I should be thanking you," Dr. Zee said. "We've had good rains this year, and my garden has developed a mind of its own, but I can only eat so many salads."

Nicholas gave a casual smile. "Well, it's very generous of you."

"*De nada.*" Dr. Zee patted Nicholas's hand, then turned abruptly to greet two older women approaching from the clearing of grass behind the marina where the old green car was parked. Something about them made my skin prickle.

One of the women was pale, tall, and thin with silver flowing hair and eyes like the sky with a storm on the horizon. She wore a long black sweater over a faded gray dress, embroidered in two columns down the front like Dr. Zee's shirt.

The other woman was darker-complected, her smoke-black hair swept up and pinned into a bun that peeked over the top of her head. Her green eyes flashed against her skin, and her painted red lips were tacked in a smile to one side. She removed a thin, yellow shawl from her shoulders and extended her hand to Dr. Zee.

"*Damas…que placer*," he said, bending to kiss it.

"The pleasure is ours, Alonzo," the first woman said, her accent sharp where the doctor's was smooth—harsh and abrupt where his was rich and rolling.

The darker woman's eyes flashed when she saw the fire, and she quickly moved to the seat Nicholas was unfolding for her.

"Well, *now* it's a pleasure," she said, her accent a strange blend of the other two.

"*Djin...*" Dr. Zee held her hand as he turned to us. "Nicholas, Cora, may I present my dear friends, Djin and Paralda."

"Gin? Like the drink?" Nicholas asked.

"If you *must* make the comparison, yes. The D is silent." Djin glowered at him. "You call this a *tropical* island, Alonzo?" she asked, moving her seat even closer to the fire than it already was.

"I think the breeze is lovely," Paralda said, her silver hair blowing off her shoulders and streaming behind her as if she had somehow called up the wind for just that effect. She took a seat and met my eyes. "Alonzo has told us so much about you."

"He has?" Now I *was* confused. We'd only just met him today.

Dr. Zee cleared his throat and gestured to the line of fish Nicholas had hung from the side of the empty chair that was waiting for him. "It looks like the waters were generous."

"For a little while." Nicholas nodded. "Until every fish in the area seemed to disappear." He took the fish off the line and arranged them on a thin piece of wood that Dr. Zee passed to him along with a small bucket of water, which he used to begin cleaning the fish. "Do you ladies live here on Snake Island?"

Djin and Paralda exchanged glances, both looking like they were trying to restrain their laughter.

"We were just visiting," Paralda said, her silver hair still seeming to blow behind her, even though the breeze had died down. "Alonzo was kind enough to ask us to dinner on our last evening here. We'll be leaving tonight."

"Where are you from?" Nicholas asked as he folded the fillets in a metallic wrapping and placed them in the fire, one of them slipping down between two pieces of wood.

"Sometimes here, sometimes there," Djin said, reaching into the fire with her bare hand to retrieve the fish. A piece of flaming wood buckled over her wrist, but no one seemed to have noticed, even though they'd been looking directly at her.

"Cora?" Nicholas asked, startling me. "Cora, what's wrong?"

"You didn't see that? You didn't see her…" I didn't need to finish the question when I saw the look on his face. The only thing that had surprised him was *my* reaction. I glanced at Dr. Zee and the two women to find all three of them looking at me…studying me.

"Didn't see what?" Nicholas asked. "Cora, are you all right?"

I turned back to him. "I'm fine… It's nothing—just the shadows from the firelight," I lied, the feeling to get away from Djin and Paralda nearly overwhelming. "I think I'm just tired."

"You've barely eaten anything today. Here," he said, taking the wrapped fish from the fire with a metal tool. He placed it on another flat piece of wood and handed it to me. "Be careful. It's still hot," he added, opening the wrapping with a series of quick tugs along the edges.

Steam rose from the fish, blurring my vision of it for a few seconds.

Paralda leaned closer to me and began waving her hand over the steam. "What a catch, don't you think,

Djin?" she said, leaning back in her seat. I jumped out of mine and fell backward at the sight of the fish, only it *wasn't* fish. It was the severed forearm of an Undine—the webbed fingers, the razor-edged fin running along the outer bone. I gasped for breath as my throat started to close.

"Cora!" Nicholas rushed to my side and lifted me back to my feet. "What happened?"

My chest burned with the effort to regulate my breaths. My throat ached with the instinct to pull in water—I needed to relax. I had to focus.

"I'm all right." I managed to choke out the words. Paralda smirked at me, and Djin raised an inky eyebrow and picked up the *fish* I had dropped from the sand. *It was a fish…* I thought. But it hadn't been. "The steam just burned my eyes."

"Tsk, tsk. Be careful, child," Dr. Zee said, crossing to get a better look at my face. "You can never be too careful around fire."

Djin laughed quietly under her breath. "Or apparently, air," she said, nodding to Paralda, who almost seemed...*proud*?

"Can you see all right?" Nicholas asked as Dr. Zee examined my face. I stepped back, out of everyone's reach.

"Yes, like I said I'm *fine*," I said, too curtly. Everyone was staring at me.

"What are you doing so far from your people, water child?" Djin asked, and I nearly fell down again in shock.

"*What*?" I shook my head at her.

"Water child?" Nicholas asked, looking just as confused as I felt.

"It doesn't matter. She was bitten by a feral. It's begun," Dr. Zee said, then turned to me. "That bite you had on your arm…where did you get it?"

"I told you—the water."

"That bite doesn't come from anything in the water," he said, looking down his long, broad nose at me.

"What's all this about? Did you say *feral*?" Nicholas asked, moving to my side again.

Dr. Zee went back to his seat. "You got yourself mixed up in a mess, *muchacho*." He sighed.

Nicholas took a step toward him. "There have been attacks back home. The news reports are calling them *feral* attacks."

"Who put you on land, child?" Paralda asked before Dr. Zee could answer.

Djin rolled her eyes. "It was Ghob, of course! Why waste any more time asking these questions?"

"She insists we call her *Luz*," Dr. Zee said with a smirk. "It's been near to a century now."

"*Luz*?" Djin's angular face pinched and tightened like she'd just eaten something rotten. "As in *light*?"

The doctor nodded. "*Mother* Light, actually."

Djin and Paralda exchanged incredulous looks and nearly fell out of their chairs laughing. They forcibly had to stop themselves so they could catch their breath.

"Are you…the only of her clan left…who knows her true name then?" Djin asked between sputters of laughter.

Alonzo snorted. "Why do you think I'm banished to this island?"

The two women erupted in laughter again, and Nicholas grabbed a stick from the fire. He held it at them like a blade.

"*Who* are you?" he asked, turning from the women to brandish the charred stick at Dr. Zee. "And who are *you* really?"

Djin coughed on the remains of her laughter, then pulled the smoldering stick from Nicholas's grasp and started *eating* the glowing end of it.

"Alonzo, tell this son of Eve to respect his elders," Paralda said as she returned to her folding chair.

The doctor heaved another sigh and turned to her. "Do you know how tiresome it is to *always* be right?" he asked. "I warned you. Did I not warn you? I said she would do it on her own."

"I must confess, I'm shocked that *Necksa* would have aligned with her."

"My mother has nothing to do with Luz!" I shouted instinctively, but regretted it when Nicholas turned to me, his surprise making me realize what I'd just said.

He held up his palms and took a few steps back from all of us. "Someone better start explaining."

I stood between Nicholas and the others, unsure what to say or do next. *You had one job, Cora…*I heard Reed's words echoing in my mind.

"*Necksa* has an heir?" Paralda asked the others. "How did she manage an heir? Who's your father, child?" she asked me, but I was tired of this game.

"How do you know me? How do you know about us!?" I shouted.

The fire flared high into the air, and Paralda's voice rang in every direction like the roar of a wave. *"Who is your father*!?"

"He died in the Gnome War!" I answered, but I had no control over the words. It was like they were just pulled directly from me.

"The *Gnome* War?" Djin laughed out loud as the fire receded. "Do you know of the Sylphs? The Salamanders?"

I shook my head hesitantly, and Djin laughed again.

"Outrage," Paralda hissed. "Did you know about this, Alonzo? Did you know Necksa told her Undines *nothing* of the Dawning?"

"How would I have known such a thing?" Dr. Zee answered.

Nicholas turned abruptly and walked toward the ship. "That's it. The shrinks were right. I'm going back," he rambled. "I'm telling them to put me in that psych ward like they should have *insisted* on doing in the first place. What kind of fool believes a prisoner could have brought a bomb on my ship? They're all fools! I'm a fool!" he continued ranting until he boarded the boat, and I couldn't hear him anymore.

I turned back to the women and Dr. Zee, unsure of what to do next—I was caught in the between place of coming and going, frozen.

Furious.

Terrified.

Djin groaned and waved two fingers in the air, then met my eyes again. "Your son of Eve will find the engine overheated. Don't worry, water child," she sighed, then narrowed her eyes at me. "Now, tell us why you're here."

Chapter 13

I ran after Nicholas, leaving Djin, Paralda, and Dr. Zee around the campfire. My head was spinning with everything they'd said…they called Mama Luz *Ghob*? What were the Sylphs and Salamanders? I had so many questions, but they would have to wait.

I ran onto the boat after Nicholas, but didn't see him at first. He wasn't behind the controls, so I turned to go below deck. I didn't get two steps down before running directly into him, nearly knocking him backward. He caught my waist and fell against the wall.

"Sorry, *sorry*…" we said at the same time. I searched his face for an indication of what he was thinking, but he was unreadable.

"Are you all right?" he finally asked. I nodded, as he cleared his throat and straightened, then walked past me back to the controls.

"Wait!" I called after him. He ignored me and started pushing a series of circles on the control board, but the ship didn't start up like it had before. "Djin told me the engine would be overheated," I said carefully.

His clear blue eyes were wide and full of questions when he looked at me, but instead of asking any of them, he just nodded absently and leaned against the wall of the small, windowed room.

He folded his arms over his chest and cut me a glare. "What did they mean when they called you *water child*?"

"I—it might have been—"

"Cora," he said abruptly. "They knew your mother. What were they talking about?"

"Nicholas, I really don't—"

"You *do* know. What are you hiding?" He closed his eyes and pushed his hands through his hair, heaving a sigh. "Are you her?"

"Am I...*who*?"

"Please. I need to know if I'm losing my mind—I need to know if I actually saw what I saw, or if..." He trailed off. "I need to know if you're the one from my ship. The one who brought me to shore." He looked at me, unguarded and seeming so alone.

My eyes started to burn, and although everything in me told me to stay quiet, to deny it all, I found myself nodding.

He slid down the wall, his forearms draped over his bent knees as he leaned his head back and closed his eyes again.

"I knew it." He almost laughed. "I knew the second I saw you. Your hair is blonde instead of silver, and your skin...the *tail*..." He did laugh now, seeming to surprise himself with the memory. He sobered after a pause and stared at me again. "But the look in your eyes was the same. There was no mistaking that."

"I'm sorry..." was all I could think to say, not quite sure how all this had happened. I scrambled to slow my mind, to think of some way I could still save Reed, not to mention myself, from Luz's—*Ghob's?*—consequences.

"Why did you come back?" he asked, visibly calmer as he glanced at my legs. "How did you...*change*?"

My mind raced again for something to say that would reset everything, but there was no way out of this. I had to tell him.

"I was trying to stop the attack on your ship that day, but there's a divide among my people," I started. "There are others, Nicholas…besides your people and mine—the Gnomes."

"*Gnomes*?" He blanched, barely restraining another laugh. "The little statues of men with mushroom hats in old ladies' gardens?"

I smiled, letting my eyes trace the lines in the planking beneath us. "Gnomes are ancient, like the Undines. We were here before humans… We were the first creations of The *Mother*." Nicholas was silent. I glanced up at him to find him staring blankly at me. "We are not the children of Eve…like you."

"*Eve*? As in Adam and Eve? Right. OK…" He got to his feet. I scrambled to block the door.

"Why would I just admit to who I was and still lie about this now?" I pressed. This stopped him. He crossed his arms over his chest again and leaned against the wall. I took a deep breath, ignoring the ache it caused. "I don't know who those women are, and it seems you don't really know Dr. Zee after all, so that means we're on the same side," I said, forgetting why I was here until the pang of guilt ran through me.

"And the rest?" he asked, fixing me in place with an icy blue gaze. "Why did you come back? *How* did you come back?"

"The siren who pulled you off your ship is called Mara. I knew you would drown before you stopped struggling against her in the water, and I couldn't let that happen." I turned away from him and looked out onto the endless sea. "I brought you to shore because you didn't deserve to die like the others who have hunted and tortured my people for centuries."

"*Mermaids*? Are we talking about mermaids here? Because that's not how our stories go," he said defensively. "Mermaids aren't real. They're the delusional fantasies of sailors who have been at sea too long. Stories meant to keep them from going stir crazy and killing each other."

I rounded on him. "Did a story keep you from dying with your crew? Was that a delusion?"

He looked at me for a long time before finally speaking again. "Then *answer* me. Why did you come back? How are you *standing* there?"

I heaved a sigh and closed my eyes, trying to find a way to avoid telling him I was here to kill him. "Because the Gnome Queen, Luz, changed me. Mara wanted her to send me here after she led the attack on your ship. *Luz* helped her. She and Mara have united the Gnomes and the Undines…they're planning a war on your people."

"So you're their queen? You're here to stop it?"

"My mother, Necksa, is the queen. I'm captain of her guard…"

"Then you're a *princess*."

"I'm a *soldier*! And I'm not here to stop their attack. I'm here to stop you!" I slipped.

His expression sharpened, his dark brows arching as he studied me for several minutes before he spoke again. "Stop *me* from what, Cora?"

It was too late. There was only the truth now. "Luz has my lieutenant—my friend—aboard her ship. She'll kill him unless…" I trailed off, scolding myself for even saying anything at all. But it was too late now. "Luz will kill him unless I kill you," I managed. "I've been given three days. Only two are left."

Nicholas stared at me and put his hands in the pockets of the white uniform pants he'd retrieved, which were now marred with dirt. "Well, this is awkward then." He smiled and turned his head but kept his eyes on me. "How was it supposed to go? Clobbering me in my sleep? A blade to my throat?"

"A kiss."

He raised his chin and smirked, despite his efforts to press his lips into a neutral line. "A *kiss*, was it…? Well, you could have killed me twice by now, Cora."

"I know," I whispered, swallowing hard as I turned again to the sea, wishing I could echo: *I'm sorry Reed. I'm so sorry*…but I didn't make a sound.

I heard Nicholas's footsteps behind me, and I didn't care. It would be better if he killed me since it was clear I wouldn't be able to kill him. I'd failed Reed. I'd failed my people. I'd failed *myself*.

Nicholas's hands moved over my shoulders, and I waited for them to tighten around my throat. Instead, his arms crossed over my shoulders and held me against him.

His rough cheek brushed my temple. "This may just be out of relief that I'm not crazy after all," he said in a quiet voice. "But even though I'm not sure how to stop two supernatural races from conquering humanity—at least not yet—I imagine that together, we could figure out how to rescue your lieutenant."

I turned into him. "You would help me? After I came here intending to *kill* you?"

"Cora…" He laughed and stroked my cheek. "If intentions were all that mattered, I'd be dead already." I flinched as he bent to kiss my forehead.

"No…" I pushed against his chest to stop him. "It's too much of a risk."

He raised a dark eyebrow and sighed, then pulled me against him. "We'll fix this," he said into my hair. "But we're going to need some help."

***

Djin, Paralda, and Dr. Zee were still sitting around the fire when we came back to it. I didn't know why I was surprised they were still there since it was clear by now the women had come because of me. They knew I was Undine before they ever sat down, and apparently, Dr. Zee was the one who told them.

I narrowed my eyes at him. "How did you know about me?" I asked. He glanced at Nicholas, who put his hand on my shoulder and waited for the answer.

"Well, now… The fish is out of the bag." Dr. Zee smiled. "I'm also an Elemental, water child. A Gnome. We recognize our own. I'm sure you felt something similar when you first saw *me*…"

I ignored his question. "If you're a Gnome, then why can you talk? Mama Luz is the only one of the Gnomes who has ever talked to us."

"Those aren't *Gnomes* she keeps on her barge. They're the slaves she fashioned from clay—silent, obedient," Dr.

Zee said spitefully. "The rest of my kind are scattered in the world. Some doing her bidding, some of us resisting. Necksa really told you *nothing* of us?"

I scowled at him. "Only that the Undines were banished from Eden for siding with the Gnomes. They told the Undines the humans wanted to make us their slaves."

Djin shook her head. "The humans didn't know anything then. The Father wanted the Elementals to *help* them. To teach them. But Ghob—*Luz*—would have none of it."

"Mama Luz was there? *Then*?" I met her eyes.

"Of course, child. The Elemental queens are immortal." Djin shook her head at me. "Your mother didn't mention that, either?"

"No," I answered.

"I told you Necksa would never forgive us." Paralda darted a glance at Djin. "I told you…"

I glared at her. "Forgive you for *what*?"

"Because we helped Ghob—*Luz*… Oh, I *cannot* call her that—" Djin rolled her eyes. "We didn't help the Undines after they were *also* banished from The Garden. But honestly, Necksa overreacted. We couldn't have given the Undines back their legs."

Anger lit in my chest. "Our history says there were still Undines on land in The Garden when they were banished. They were trapped there! This was *your* fault?" I demanded. "What *are* you!?"

"Aren't you listening?" Djin started. "It *wasn't* our fault that Ghob misled you mother. In fact—"

She was silenced when Paralda held up one hand to her. "But it *was* our fault that we let Ghob back in to retrieve the discarded forbidden fruit. We did nothing for Necksa or her Undines. Tell her the whole story, Djin."

I pressed my teeth together to keep from screaming. "Who *are* you?"

Paralda held her hand delicately over her chest. "I am the Queen of the Sylphs." She paused. "We are of the air, and the Salamanders," she gestured to Djin, "are of the great fire. Djin is their queen. We are also Elementals, like the Gnomes and the Undines."

"*Why* did you help Luz? Why did you help her but not my mother?"

Djin took another bite from the smoldering stick from the fire and changed the flames into the image of lush trees. With a wave of her hand, flowering bushes appeared behind four large, golden gates. She swallowed and cleared her throat. "Not long after Ghob and the Undines were expelled, Paralda and I were *ordered* by The Father to hide The Garden." She snorted again, then turned to Paralda, interrupting herself. "Do you remember that angel, Uriel, patrolling the gates with his flaming sword? Back and forth marching like some kind of wind-up toy…"

Paralda laughed and leaned toward me conspiratorially. "He was rather new then. Wanted to make a good impression."

Dr. Zee shook his head like he'd heard the story a hundred times and wasn't interested in hearing it again.

Djin saw him and sighed. "Anyway, you can imagine, there was very little time between Adam dropping the fruit and the thunderous order to hide The Garden. There were only so many risks we could take... Ghob could make a new Garden from the seed of that fruit, but it wasn't as if there were any *fish tail* trees scattered about that would have benefited Necksa's people."

"*Djin,*" Paralda scolded. I was starting to understand why my mother had never spoken of these women before. In just this short time with them, I already couldn't stand them.

Dr. Zee nodded. "Ghob could have given the Undines back their legs to come and go again as they pleased on land, but she feared it would bring attention to her new Garden, and all would be punished."

Paralda leaned forward, extending a long, slim hand to me. I pulled away from her. "Your mother ordered the Undines to attack the Gnome ships shortly after that. It was the only justice she could have since she could not reach the Sylphs in the air or the Salamanders in the sky's great fire."

"And this became the Gnome War..." I said to myself, fully understanding the visceral hatred the Undines had harbored for Mama Luz for so long. But I didn't understand why my mother was so careful to protect her now...or what could have happened to bring about the treaty we held with them.

Djin sighed, evidently bored with all of this. "There, you have your history lesson. Now, tell us how you've come to be on land."

I glared at her, but thought better of it.

"You didn't help my mother years ago," I said carefully. "Make it right by helping me now."

Chapter 14

I explained to Paralda, the Sylph queen, and to Djin, the Salamander queen, about Reed…about Mara and the pending war Luz was trying to wage against the humans. It was hard to understand her motives, especially since she'd actually *regained* Eden, sort of.

"Luz wants more than that now," Dr. Zee said, finishing the last of his fish.

I nodded. "She's convinced the Undines of the Depths that the humans stole our world. She's been recruiting them to take it back."

"Apparently, one boat at a time," Nicholas said with a scowl.

"But now there are other soldiers in the war she's mounting," Dr. Zee added, glancing again at my arm. The dark outline of the bite mark was still visible, even though the burns from the electrical restraints were completely gone. "She's creating them. *Ferals*—something between humans and Elementals that are both susceptible to infections like humans, but like Elementals, cannot be killed by them."

"How is she doing that?" Nicholas asked.

Djin passed her hand over the flames, which only showed one tree now, the others having fallen away with the dying fire. "She's created another Tree of Life…"

"The *Tree of Life*? Adam and Eve again?" Nicholas asked, his expression dubious.

"It never ceases to amaze me how the children of Eve refuse to believe, even as the proof is in front of them," Djin said gently, her voice almost sympathetic.

Her condescension wasn't lost on Nicholas. He gave her a steely look and clenched his jaw.

"I want to stop her, but before I can do that, I have to save Reed," I reminded them all.

"And yourself," Djin said, looking again into the fire, which had taken the shape of a boat on the sea.

I glared at Djin, remembering the severed Undine arm she and Paralda conspired to make me hallucinate. "If you could read the fire the whole time, why did you bother with your *games* earlier?"

"The fire only shows the story you start to tell, water child." She gave me a slow, closed lip smile that made my skin crawl.

Nicholas turned to me." What else happens in two days?"

"I don't even know. Not really. Mama Luz just said the *earth would see us*—Reed and me."

Djin poked at the flames, making them jump and recede in the glowing coals. "Seems she'll let your friend bake in the sun. And when the last of your water marks dries…" She tilted her head to watch the fire from a new angle. "Old *Mama Luz* will send her scattered Gnomes to do the same to you."

"But I'm human now. How is that possible if…?" I trailed off, ashamed to even think it, let alone say it out loud. I cleared my throat and tried again. "She said I could only go back to being Undine if…I killed Nicholas. If I spilled his blood in the sea."

Nicholas drew in a long, slow breath.

"Seems there was fine print she didn't mention," Dr. Zee added, the creases in his forehead deepening when he raised his eyebrows at me.

Nicholas scrubbed his hands over his face, then got to his feet. "What if we gave her what she wants? Just spill my blood into the sea."

"No! I can't—" I started to protest, but he held his hands up to stop me.

"This can work," he said, almost to himself as he pulled his knife from his belt and ran to the shoreline.

"Nicholas!" I called after him, but he didn't stop until he splashed knee-high into the water. When I caught up to him, he'd already slashed his forearm and was dripping his blood into the surf.

"How much did she say you had to spill?" he asked, balling his hand into a fist to make the blood flow faster.

"Stop this!" I took the knife from him and cut off the edge of my tank top, then tied it around his arm.

"It's done then. What's supposed to happen now?" he asked, making my chest suddenly feel hollow.

*Da water will make ya Undine again...*Mama Luz's words echoed in my head. I looked down at my legs, equally terrified they would change back into a tail and that they wouldn't.

Nothing happened.

Nothing changed.

"It didn't work," I whispered, both relieved and afraid of what that meant. Nicholas's blood had been spilled, technically, but the water knew somehow that he wasn't dead. Would Mama Luz know too? Would the water betray me and tell her?

The irrational thoughts swam through my head, but realizing they were irrational didn't make them stop.

"How do you know it didn't work?" Nicholas asked, holding his arm. The blood was already soaking through the thin fabric of the torn, red tank top and dripped again into the water.

"Because I haven't changed back," I said, afraid to take my eyes from my legs.

"What have you done to yourself, son of Eve?" Djin called from the shore, half-laughing, half-exasperated, alongside Paralda, who looked at us both with pity.

Nicholas cleared his throat. "It didn't work…" he said, his voice sounding far away.

My legs started to burn, but it wasn't heat, it was a frigid burn. "Something is wrong!" I shouted, falling backward into the silt with a splash. The water froze my hands, my wrists, my hips—everything it touched.

I scrambled backward onto the sand, and finally, the frigid burning started to fade. Nicholas fell to his knees in the sand at my side.

"What is it? What's happening?" he asked, scanning me up and down. He gripped my shoulders, held my face. "Cora!"

His blood dripped over my sweatpants, the spots disappearing into the dark fabric.

"I'm all right. It stopped burning. It stopped…" I said, surprising myself that I was so out of breath.

Nicholas's eyes widened as they darted to my throat.

He let go of my face and moved back, watching me in horror. "What's happening to her?"

I brought my hands to my throat and felt around frantically, stopping all at once when my fingertips touched the ends of the second line. It seemed to sink until it was gone, leaving nothing but smooth skin behind, and only one raised line remained on each side.

"There's only one now," I said under my breath. "There's only one line." I looked up at Djin and Paralda. "Does that mean I only have one day left now?"

Dr. Zee picked up a fistful of sand and let it spill from his fingers. Paralda held out her hand, slowing the sand until it finally stopped, frozen in the shape of an Undine held above the water. But the sand above this did not stop. It expanded into a circle…a sun that kept expanding until it consumed the suspended Undine. Afterward, all the sand fell at once to the ground.

Nicholas scooped up the fallen sand and let it slip through his fingers. "That was you, wasn't it?" he asked quietly. "That was a message…I did this to you."

*…de earth will see ya, water child. It will see you and de fishy-man…*I heard Mama Luz's voice faintly on the water, washed away only by the sound of a slow, rolling laugh that blew over us on the breeze.

"No," I said, beginning to shiver. "It was Reed. She was showing me what she would do to Reed."

Paralda gripped my arm and lifted me to my feet with a strength I wouldn't have anticipated given her long, delicate build. "It's not safe for you here anymore, Cora. Or for your son of Eve."

"What do you mean?" Nicholas asked, getting to his feet.

"Consider it a warning," Djin said. "One day instead of two before she sends the hidden ones for you. For both of you now."

"How do we stop them?" I asked, trying to keep my teeth from chattering.

Nicholas didn't give them a chance to answer. "How do you kill an immortal queen?"

***

Dr. Zee helped us load the ship with the supplies he brought: food, clothes, some tools. If we were going to save Reed, we would need to sail back to the sandbar, back to the island where the Lawless first attacked Nicholas's ship. It was suicide with the Lawless Undine just below the surface, but Paralda promised she would call up Sylphs in the form of winds to toss the sea once we were close enough, and Djin promised to call down Salamanders in the form of lightning.

These ambassadors would help us sink Mama Luz's barge, scattering everyone aboard beneath the waves. If it worked, the Lawless Undines would be helpless to resist their natures. We only had to trust that the Elemental queens would be watching and would know when we needed them most.

But if they didn't do their part, we would be lost.

"We need a backup plan to sink that boat," I said as we hit the open water.

Nicholas chuckled. "Exactly what I was thinking. I'm not counting on a magical thunderstorm to just appear *when we need* it."

"I could sink it... after I changed back," I said, my mind racing.

He turned the steering wheel, making us arc away from Snake Island toward the darkening horizon. "Djin said the Gnomes would be coming. That the *earth would see* you."

"But she also said I would turn back into an Undine when my last watermark disappeared," I added, remembering the flames dancing in the campfire as she described it to us. "The Gnomes don't know that *I know* this. They'll be expecting to find me on land, stranded and helpless."

He shook his head adamantly at the horizon. "You would be alone in the water surrounded by the Lawless. It's too much of a risk—unless..." He trailed off, then turned to me. "Unless I ram this boat into Luz's barge and sink them both."

"You think it's better for *you* to be alone in the water, surrounded by the Lawless?" I asked, incredulous.

"No...we can set the collision course and jump into a life raft in the opposite direction."

"And then I can swim toward the wreckage," I said, imagining. "The Lawless will be too busy attacking Luz and her minions to notice me. I can free Reed..."

"And I'll row to the island," Nicholas nodded. "It would be over." His eyes fixed on the horizon. "Where would you go then, Cora?"

I wasn't sure how to answer him. Nothing would be the same, even if everything went perfectly. There would be too many Lawless to subdue, especially in the long term. Even if we were able to get them to kill Mama Luz, the seeds of war had already been sown, and it would only be a matter of time before the conflict found us in the Southern Depths.

How did this happen? I thought. *How did the Undines drift so far apart...?*

Chapter 15

We sailed for the better part of the night, finally stopping on the far side of *Scrapper Island*, as Nicholas called it, although he said its real name was *Samana Cay*. In all the times I hid along the sandbar in The Shallows and watched the guards unload the prisoners, I never saw them come to the shore again. They just made their way into the forest as the soldiers instructed... No campfires, no one walking on the beach, I never even saw anyone fishing.

"This is the eastern chip—the little cay," Nicholas explained as he let the boat drift toward the shore. "We'll anchor here for the night. Scrapper Island is a few hours that way on the other side of the straight, but I don't want to try to navigate that in the dark."

He didn't explain, but he didn't have to. Even if he were talking about avoiding the thickets of high-reaching coral beds between the islands, I couldn't help but think he must be feeling some hesitation at approaching this island again. The shallow waters here were *my home*, and all I could see was the carnage of the Lawless attacking his ship every time I closed my eyes.

"How much farther is it to your land?" I asked, trying to clear my mind as we made our way to the ship's railing.

He looked out on the black water. "Oh, we're a good distance from The Grind."

"That's the name of your land? The *Grind*?"

"Not officially." He laughed a little. "It's just another way to say that it's hard to get ahead there...to be successful. Maine isn't what it used to be."

"What's *Maine*?"

"I keep forgetting you're...*different*," he said, still smiling. "Maine is a state—a piece of land—pretty far north. It would take about three months to sail there from here." He crossed to sit in the net strung up behind us and held out his arm to me. "Come on. It's called a hammock. It's like a bed."

"You *sleep* in that?"

"Sure, come on."

I made my way inside the netting, nearly falling out twice. "What's *months*?" I asked, finally still again.

His dark eyebrows jumped. "Months? All right, months..." He nodded decidedly. "Months are time, you know? I guess three of them would be like ninety sunsets, if that makes sense?"

I shook my head, confused, but not about how long he meant. "Ninety? But you were already in...*Maine* when the guard put me on your boat, and it hadn't been that many sunsets since…" I trailed off, not wanting to bring up the unfortunate circumstances surrounding our *first* meeting.

He took in a deep breath and turned his eyes toward the sea. "I'd sent a distress signal before the attack got out of hand," he said evenly. "Two helicopters—um...*flying ships* with long blades on top. They were at Scrapper Island the next day to take my crew back to Maine."

"I've seen *helicopters* before. There are several beyond the boundary waters," I added, intending to offset the heaviness, but only wound up adding to it.

He nodded. "This area is known for that," he said seriously. "It's one corner of the Bermuda Triangle. Planes, helicopters, ships—something just...*swallows* them." He turned to me, his eyes full of questions he wasn't asking, but it was clear what he wanted to know.

"The Lawless brought down several ships in my lifetime alone, both from the water and from the skies," I confessed to him. "It's the song they sing."

He narrowed his eyes, but not in anger. "*Planes*?"

"It would take a school of Undines for the sound to reach it, but it could, depending on the size of the school. It could travel the length of several hundred whales."

"Maybe through the *water*, but..." Nicholas started, then shook his head and seemed to abandon the thought. He pushed his free hand through his dark hair and closed his eyes. "Anyway..." He sighed. "Since Maine is a three-month trip, how did *you* appear on the Weigh Station barge a few days after you saved me? You couldn't have swum that fast."

I didn't answer him right away. Instead, I just listened to him breathe until I could think of the simplest thing to tell him. At this point, it wound up being the truth.

"I wish I knew," I said, not sure if it was even loud enough for him to hear me. "Mama Luz put me in a rowboat with one of her minions. He rowed into a fog, and we came out the other side on the shore of your... Maine *Grind* land."

He drew in a deep breath and let it out slowly. "So much doesn't make any sense. I keep wondering what else is out there now. What else has been there the whole time, and I never even knew."

I nodded because I felt the same way.

"I didn't even know the Sylph and Salamander Elementals existed, let alone that the queens were immortal. I thought my mother was just telling stories of our past about the Gnomes, but she was actually *there*. She was part of the stories." I said, one thought crashing into the next like a wave that was starting to fall. "I don't know what that means for me—if I'm like them, immortal...or if I'm something else. What if there are no others like me?" I thought out loud.

He stroked my cheek, the moonlit water reflecting in his eyes when I turned to him. He smiled slowly and lowered his forehead to mine. "No one could be like you, Cora. I couldn't have imagined you if I'd tried."

***

I hadn't realized I'd fallen asleep until I heard a whale echo, but it was so distant I wondered if I'd only dreamed it. I opened my eyes to a smoke-colored sky, not quite morning, but no longer the pitch of night. The echo came again, and this time, I was sure I was awake.

I raised my head to scan the deck, and carefully stood up when Nicholas turned to his side. I walked toward the railing, pulled by the whale song, which wasn't a distress call. It was an announcement. Something to say, *I'm coming*.

I gripped the railing and peered into the dark water below, but I didn't hear the echo again. Instead, a hand wrapped around my mouth from behind as another wrapped around my arms, pinning them to my sides.

"Don't scream!" a voice whisper-yelled in my ear. "It's all right. It's all right now…"

I struggled against the vise closing around me, but the arms just lifted me off my feet. I instinctively tried to sweep my captor's legs out with my tail but only wound up flailing my own legs backward. I bent forward as hard and as quickly as I could, which flipped the man over my shoulder and against the railing.

"Nicholas!" I shouted as I ran back toward the hammock, but three of Mama Luz's Gnomes were already struggling to bind his arms.

"Cora! Get off the boat!" he shouted, but there was no way I was going to abandon him. I started to run toward the Gnomes. If I could knock one of them down, it would give Nicholas a chance to see what he was fighting. I only got about two or three strides when I was pulled off my feet by a strong arm that almost crushed my ribs as it squeezed the air from my chest.

I struggled again, but in the process, we fell over the railing and into the water. We hit hard, the skim feeling like the decking of a ship against my face and arms. My ears rang, and nausea bloomed in my chest as water rushed down my throat.

The freezing burn of the water ignited all over my skin again, a hundred thousand little stabbing sensations all at once, and we just kept sinking farther and farther down until I felt the scraping of a coral bed against my thigh.

I screamed involuntarily, losing any remaining air I had as the arm around my waist tightened again, jerking me up and up and up until I broke through the skim. I coughed, gasping for breath, but there was no chance to get my bearings as I was pulled to the shoreline with the same force as if I'd been caught in a net. I tried to twist again, but found my legs and hips pinned over a someone's shoulder. My arms were free, so I clenched my hands into fists and began beating at the body that was apparently carrying me. It was like hitting a *rock wall* and did about the same amount of damage to it. I tried to push against it, to launch myself back into the sea, but even with the slippery water, there was no breaking free of the arms closed over the backs of my legs.

"Nicholas!" I shouted, hoping I would hear him reply. Hoping the Gnomes hadn't managed to subdue him, but I didn't hear anything but my own shouting.

The man carrying me fell onto the beach, and whatever wind I had left was knocked out of me when I fell hard on the sand. I coughed violently, gasping for air that wouldn't enter my lungs. My throat burned. Everything burned.

"Cora...*listen*." I heard my name, breathless from the man hovering over me, pinning my arms to the ground.

I gasped again, trying to summon enough air to shout in his face, but nothing came. Partly out of panic, I drove my knees up and into his side, knocking him free of me. I scrambled to my feet and turned back toward the water, hoping I could find my way in the dark...hoping there was a dragnet on the side of the boat. I couldn't remember. I couldn't remember anything.

I was almost to the water when I was pulled off my feet again, this time, backward onto the sand. The man crawled over me, his weight pinning my hips to the ground. He pressed my shoulders into the sand so hard it felt like rods had been driven through them straight into the earth.

"No!" I shouted because it was the only word I had enough breath left to form.

"Cora! Cora, it's all right! Please, just listen!"

I stopped struggling. He'd said my name. He'd said it on the ship, I realized, but I hadn't really heard him then. Mama Luz's minions didn't talk. They never talked. They were strong like this man, but they didn't speak.

"Who are you?" I choked. "Get off me!"

I bucked under him with the last remnant of strength I could find. It wasn't enough to have moved him, but he moved anyway and sat at my side. He pushed his light hair from his face and gripped my shoulders.

I saw the shape of him before I recognized him. His angular features, his fair skin—his nearly white hair and eyebrows and long, sharp nose. His wide mouth was held open, panting for breath with no trace of the smirk I'd come to know. He didn't wear a shirt, and his broad chest, his arms, every part of him seemed carved and fixed in stone there on the beach.

Moonlight glinted off a small glass bead of some kind that was hooked to the spear strap across his chest. His torn half-pants were bunched and wrinkled in the folds of his hips, and his legs—*his legs*—were rounded with woven muscles that flexed and hardened as I watched them pull under his body when he leaned toward me. He shook my shoulders and met my eyes, his, piercing and bright green as he searched my face.

"Cora…" he said, this time softly.

I blinked, and then I blinked again. "Reed?" I whispered.

"Yes, yes…" he laughed, his deep voice breaking as he pulled me into him, crushing my ribs again. He loosened his grip when he felt the air rush out of me, then brought his hands to my face. "Sorry… It's just different…moving like this. Are you all right?"

I didn't know what to say. There were so many questions that I couldn't even extract one from the churning mangle of them in my brain. I shook my head at him in wild disbelief. "Reed…?" I said, still not sure anything in front of me was real.

"It's me, Cora. It's me. I'm here." I stared at him, touched his face. His hand covered mine and pressed my palm flat against his cheek. "We can go home now," he said, moving his other hand into my hair." Do you trust me?" I nodded, and he leaned in, drawing me to him until his lips pressed gently to mine.

Chapter 16

Reed pulled back slowly, and I wasn't sure what was happening. I didn't even know what to ask him because we were only…friends, *soldiers*…weren't we?

"Sorry," he whispered, his hand still in my hair. His other hand folded around mine and brought it to his chest. "I had to do that to start everything over—I mean…not like I *wouldn't* have… It was just…"

I shook my head to stop his babbling. He was here. *Here.* And he was alive.

"What are you talking about?" I asked, still a little dizzy." Start what over?" I tried to get my bearings again." Are you all right? How are you here?"

He took a deep breath and blew it out slowly. "Mama Luz knows where you are, Cora. Earlier today, a wave came from nowhere and hit her ship. It gave me my strength back, and I'd almost cut myself free, but then she started ranting about how she was going to find a way to kill you—she said you'd cost her the Undine Guard if Mara found out that you were *helping* the captain now," he rambled, then looked down at the sand. "I pretended to be angry about it," he added, but from the tone of his voice, I didn't completely believe he had pretended anything. "I didn't know where to find you, so I told her to send *me* to kill him. That's all Mara wanted, right?"

"You were *with* the Gnomes just now? Where did they take him, Reed?"

He shook his head at me like he was struggling to understand, but then he abandoned trying. "They're holding him on the boat. Cora, are you listening to me?"

"Why would Mama Luz have agreed to this after Mara insisted on sending me? Mama Luz could have killed him herself if his death is all that mattered."

"No, that's what I'm trying to tell you. She can't kill anything and neither can her Gnomes. She was screaming at the sky about it after the wave hit—she needs the Undines, Cora. We're hunters, the Gnomes are farmers. They're not *able* to kill."

"She never could have killed you?" I whispered.

"Apparently not, but she can make us suffer. I don't know the whole story, but she was desperate to end all this before Mara brought back the Guard from the Southern Depths. I don't think Mama Luz plans to tell her how it all went down."

"How all *what* went down? You're not making any sense!"

He pulled the sheath of his short spear to the front of his chest. "Look, just wait here for me, and then we can go home, all right?"

"*Wait* for you?" I said, finally realizing what he was planning. "Do you think I'm just going to let you walk back onto that boat to kill him?"

He narrowed his eyes at me, genuinely lost. "I kissed you to *take* that burden from *you*, Cora, but it will only last if that captain's blood hits the water *after* I kill him. I should have told you that in the first place, but I just—look…do you want to die here, stranded once Mama Luz changes us back to Undines? I'm taking you *home*." Reed pulled his short spear from its sheath and started for the boat.

"Stop!" I jumped to my feet and stepped in front of him. "There are things you don't know about Mama Luz! Can't you see this isn't right?"

He narrowed his eyes at me, confused and almost pleading as he shook his head." What I see is you putting one human's life before your own. Before mine. Before all the Undines'. *You're* the one who called his kind monsters. Now *get out* of my way so I can end this before we have a civil war on our hands."

"No!" I shouted again. "The humans are not what I thought. Not all of them anyway. None of this is the way we thought, Reed. The humans never wanted us to be their slaves. To them, *we're* the monsters, and it's all because of Mama Luz!" I pressed my hands flat against his chest and pushed him back.

"Even if that's true, we don't have time right now to fix any of it, all right? *Get out of my way*, Cora! We're running out of time!"

I turned and ran for the boat. Reed was strong, but I knew he was still far from agile on his new legs. I didn't risk looking back to see if he was gaining on me, I just boarded the boat and pulled the stairs up behind me so he couldn't follow.

The sun was starting to come up, and in the dim light, I saw the *broken pieces* of one of Mama Luz's creations. His limbs cracked, his body shattered to pieces like a crushed shell. I ran past it all toward the upper deck where I saw the other two slaves restraining Nicholas, one of them desperately trying to wrap a rope around his neck. I dove for that one's legs, but he only stumbled as a jolt of pain ran through my shoulders.

Nicholas flipped the slave behind him over his shoulder and tossed him into the one I'd tried to tackle. Both tumbled to the decking, and Nicholas wove the rope quickly around them. He hit something that looked like a small wheel, and the rope jerked them overboard as it brought up the dragnet. He quickly cut the rope, making Mama Luz's slaves drop to the water below.

"Let's go!" Nicholas shouted as we moved back into the small control room. He started the ship engine, which screeched and rattled everything around us.

"It didn't sound like that before!" I shouted over the noise.

"It's the anchor. It must be caught on something." Nicholas shook his head and pushed down on a lever next to the wheel. The engine screamed again, and with an abrupt jerk, we were moving freely.

Fear lodged in my chest for Reed. I could only hope he was still too unfamiliar with his legs to have made his way back into the water so soon after I boarded the boat.

"What happened?" I asked after a pause.

"We either lost the anchor or that reef lost a branch," Nicholas answered, pushing the ship to full speed. The small island fell away in the distance, and with it, Reed.

The sun broke over the horizon, and in the same instant, the last water marks on my throat started to burn.

"What's happening?" I yelled, my hands flying to them. Like the others, they, too, seemed to sink until there was nothing remaining but smooth skin, and I was terrified of what might happen next.

"Are you all right? Cora!" Nicholas reached for me with one hand while the other held fast to the wheel. I grabbed his hand, and he pulled me to him. "Can you talk!?"

"Yes," I answered, the reality of my voice somehow calming the panic that just ripped through me. "It's gone…" I said to myself, trying to piece together what Reed had said back on the shore.

"What's gone?" Nicholas shouted over the roaring engine. We were going so fast, the spray of the water hit the windows like it might break through, and the noise was almost deafening. I stretched to show him my throat, sure I wouldn't be able to speak loudly enough to explain. His hold around my waist loosened as his eyes widened, the blue igniting in the sunrise. He let me go, risking a glance at my legs, and I knew we were both thinking the same thing. I was out of time, and it was still two hours to Mama Luz's barge.

Nicholas shifted a lever after a quick look behind us, and the boat slowed. There wasn't much light yet, but there was enough to see that the island was barely visible now. The waters below us would be teeming with Lawless Undines, but as long as we didn't slow down significantly, they couldn't take the boat. At least, I didn't think I would be susceptible to their echoes, which is what caused ships' crews to stop monitoring their controls in the first place.

"Are you all right?" he asked, scanning me.

"I think so. The burning stopped, and I feel…the same," I answered, darting a glance at my legs.

Nicholas let out a deep breath. "All right, good. Do you know why they attacked us *now*? We were supposed to have one more day."

"Because Mama Luz knows I'm not going to kill you. Reed said a wave hit her ship, and she just started ranting about it."

"Reed? Your lieutenant? The *prisoner*?"

"Yes… He saw an opportunity when he heard her shouting about how she couldn't actually kill anyone. It's a long story, but Mama Luz can only kill others with the help of the Undines…" I trailed off, trying to decide how to say the rest carefully." He came to kill you because I wouldn't. That's the only way Mama Luz can guarantee she'll have control of our Guard. Mara, the Undine I saved you from that night, wants you dead."

Nicholas's dark eyebrows jumped. He pulled a hand down over his face and nodded." All right. But he's your lieutenant. Why wouldn't he just go rally your Guard himself against Mara and Mama Luz? Why wouldn't he just take charge and stop all this?"

I took a deep breath, feeling a wave of guilt rising in my stomach. "Because he came to find *me*…" I shook my head, remembering how he lost his promotion to squadron captain all because he came to find me for the ceremony. "He has a bad habit of doing that."

Nicholas was quiet at first but seemed to decide something after a minute.

"Why didn't you go with him?" he asked, glancing at me quickly. "This all could have been over for you."

"Mama Luz is putting together an army of *Ferals* on land. You heard Djin. There will be war above, and if Luz manages to take the Undines in the water, we'll have a civil war below. There's no way out of this for me."

"All the more reason for you to go back. Your people need you, Cora."

"And I need them. But I think I also need you," I blurted before I could second guess myself. It's what I felt, and I was tired of just pushing that aside to keep up with what I was *supposed* to do.

Nicholas threw another lever, and the engine noise finally subsided as we began to coast.

He started to reach for me, but was pulled backward, grabbed from behind by Reed, who pinned his arms and brought his short spear to Nicholas's throat.

"Reed!" I gasped, scanning the small control room for how he could have gotten in. It was then that I realized the window behind us was broken—he must have caught enough of the dragnet to climb aboard and break the window when the engine was roaring at full speed.

"You need *him*?" Reed asked, his green eyes fiery as he glared at me and pushed the spear against Nicholas's throat until it drew blood. "He's *human*, Cora! How long have you preached to everyone about what monsters they are!?"

"I didn't *know*," I said, trying so hard to keep my voice level. "It was all a mistake—just listen to me." I took a step toward him, but stopped when he pressed his blade into Nicholas's throat again, now drawing a steady trickle of blood. I held up my palms. "There are others out there, Reed. Other Elementals. Sylphs from the air and Salamanders from fire. I met their queens. Mama Luz wants the world for herself. She tricked my mother once, and she's trying to do it all again. She will just betray us. *Please*! Let him go."

"I don't care about her, Cora! I don't care what she did centuries ago!" Reed shouted so loudly the vein in his neck jumped. "She can track you now, do you know that? It wasn't a human that bit you. It was one of her new monsters. Halfbreeds. She has *men* making them, Cora."

Nicholas grabbed Reed's arm and bent forward, freeing himself enough to drive Reed back against the wall with his own short spear angled at his ribs.

"No!" I shouted. Nicholas looked up for just a second —enough for Reed to land a blow to the back of his head, which knocked him unconscious.

"Nicholas!" I started to run to his side, but Reed got there first, grabbing a fistful of Nicholas's hair as he repositioned his short spear at his throat.

"Come back with me, Cora." Reed's expression was equal parts fury and pleading." We can figure out what to do next like we've always done, but this isn't our problem. I know you think it is, but the humans did this to themselves. It's *their* war, and if Luz wants to take the Lawless down with her, so be it."

"I can't let that happen."

"It's *already* happening, Cora!" Reed laughed, exasperated. "There are thousands of Lawless who are loyal to Luz now even without the Guard. Once Mara gives her that, there will be no hope. Bring the Guard back to the Southern Depths with me, where we can regroup."

"I just need to talk to the Lawless. I just need a little time. We have a plan!"

Reed laughed again, this time cynically. "Luz will spend the rest of eternity keeping you one breath away from dying if I don't kill him and put his blood in the water. That's an easy choice for me, Cora." Reed shook his head, his nearly white brows darting together as he jabbed the blade into Nicholas's throat and pulled it out quickly." I thought it would have been an easy one for you too."

Chapter 17

"Nicholas!" I shouted, falling to his side when Reed stood up. There was so much blood pouring through my fingers as I tried to cover the wound. I pulled what was left of my tank top over my head and pressed it to his throat." It's all right... You're going to be all right..." I tried to keep my voice level. Tried to keep the tears from blinding me. "What have you done!?" I screamed at Reed as time screeched to a halt.

He sheathed the bloody blade and pulled the cork from *what I thought* was a glass bead hooked to his spear strap. He quickly drank whatever was inside, then jerked me up and pinned me against his body. I pushed against him, but he kissed me hard, forcing the thick and bitter liquid into my mouth until I couldn't help but swallow it.

My throat started burning inside and out. "What...did you...do to me?" I coughed, struggling to pull in a full breath.

He loosened his grip enough to bring one of his hands to my face. "I'm sorry. It was the only way—I have to bring you back."

I spit in his face, then tried to kick him. Had he been only human, even a trained human, I would have been able to overpower him, but there was nothing I could do when he wrapped his other arm around my hips and pinned my arms against his stomach again, and *again*, I could barely breathe, let alone move.

"I will never forgive you for this!" I yelled. He flinched, but quickly reset his hard expression and lifted me off my feet. A breath later, he'd launched us both through the door, over the railing, and back into the sea.

The water burned everything from the outside of my body in—not frigid this time, but a searing, stabbing pain down my back, my arms, my hips, and legs. My chest and throat tightened as I tried to scramble back to the surface, but Reed's hold was impossible to break.

I heard my muffled screams in the water, pressed and trapped under the weight of the sea that was drowning them. Forcing them to die in my throat. To change.

I tried to pull in a breath but instead felt the water rush through my *gills.* The burning faded. The tightness in my chest loosened, and finally, so did Reed's arms. He shimmered in front of me, the armored scales over his stomach and torso catching the morning light. He drew his short spear, and I watched Nicholas's blood dissipate in the water.

"Cora," he echoed, the sound rich and full in my ears, in my chest… His voice moved through me, and it wasn't until this moment that I understood the feeling I'd been missing since Mama Luz took my echo.

The fins on my arms had returned, as had the armored scales over my chest and stomach. I saw all of this, but it was only when the fins of my tail rolled out in the gentle current that I fully realized what had happened.

"You *killed* him…" I echoed to Reed, the image playing out in my mind again. My shock turned to outrage. "You killed him so you could change me!" He started to respond, but I shook my head at him and darted for the surface. I broke through the skim, but I couldn't see the boat in any direction anymore. It had been coasting. How could it have disappeared in so little time?

Unless this all took longer than it seemed? How long was I under? How long had it taken to change back into an Undine?

I felt like I was losing my mind and screamed as loudly as I could. It sounded like a screeching bird, just like Reed's airborne voice aboard Mama Luz's boat.

Reed...

I dove back through the skim and rammed his chest with my shoulder. He didn't have enough time to completely brace for the blow, and flipped backward a few times trying to right himself.

"Cora! Listen to me!" he echoed, swimming toward me, but I didn't want to listen to him. I wanted to hurt him.

"You *killed* him!" I echoed, the sound already thinning. "You don't get to decide what I am, Reed! Nobody gets to decide what I am!"

Reed wrapped his arms around me. I pounded on his chest and tried to push him away, but he only held me more tightly.

"I'm sorry. Cora, I had to kill him," he kept saying. "I couldn't let her hunt you. I wasn't going to let Mama Luz torture you too, do you understand? I'm not sorry for that, Cora." His echo was heavy and wide-reaching. It surrounded us, folded in on us, and I wouldn't let it. I jerked my tail up and into his side, breaking his hold on me.

"He was innocent! Even if I couldn't do it—if I *wouldn't*... I wanted to save you *both*, can't you see that?"

I explained, trying to find my way through it, to find the logic that would make it all clear, but there were too many blurred lines. There was only one clear answer. "Mara was right about me," I echoed. "My mother was right…I'm not a warrior."

Reed took my hands. "Cora, stop. You're Captain of the Guard. This isn't over."

"I can't lead! You would have died because of me— because I couldn't kill him, Reed!" I echoed a piercing, shrill wail that shot through the water. "But I didn't want him to die, and I hate you for killing him!" I pulled away, shaking my head. "And I don't even know what that means now because I couldn't have lived with myself if the price of *his* life would've been yours…" I babbled, delirious with rage and grief.

"I know," Reed echoed, low and gentle. He closed his arms around me. "I know, Cora."

Everything inside me felt like it was tearing loose and falling away, floating free and lost, desperate to find its way back again.

"I'm sorry," I echoed to Reed, to Nicholas, to everyone I'd failed. "I couldn't…I just couldn't…" I trailed off because it was too painful to think. It was too heavy to carry.

Reed tried to hold me more tightly, echoing that it was all OK and that he understood, but he didn't understand. Nobody could understand.

I pushed away from him and darted into the deep. Lightning lit the world above, and the resounding crash of thunder drilled down through the water until it rattled my bones. Another flash, another crash drove me deeper until I couldn't see Nicholas's blood rushing over my hands, until I couldn't see anything but the darkness. I swam *deeper* until I couldn't hear Reed's echo, until I couldn't hear anything but the sound of my own heartbeat in the stillness of the abyss pressing in all around me. No up, no down. Only nothingness, *everywhere.*

A pain in my chest started dull and low, but it began growing and spreading until it made its way to my throat. It pushed up and up until it pushed out, a single bubble that seemed to glow.

It grew slowly and positioned itself under me. I moved off it, dove down again, but it chased me and again, buoyed me up. This happened over and over until I thought I would collapse with the effort of one more evasive dive, so I stopped. I let it carry me *just long enough*, I told myself, until I could regroup to fight my way back down again.

But I couldn't muster that much strength. Slowly, the light returned, the flashes, the sun rays, and so did the thunder. So did Reed's desperate, haunting location echoes.

I floated to the skim, which was being pummeled by rain. Dark clouds churned in the sky above as I lay on my back, my arms drifting away from me at my sides. Lightning bolts shot across the sky like a charging army, disappearing as quickly as they came and leaving a fiery imprint in their wake like a memory.

"Water child," I heard in the gale—the low, resounding hum of wind through the rain. "Cora of The Shallows..."

The bubble that brought me to the surface popped next to me, and from it, Paralda rose over me and extended her long, slim hand. I reached for it this time, but she just drifted into the sky. In her place, three tornadoes tore away from the roiling clouds and made their way down to me, lightening and thinning the closer they got.

They each changed into a figure—two men and a woman. They were pale, silver like the Undine, but translucent instead of iridescent.

"Who are you?" I whispered, my airborne voice like a whistle on the wind.

"Sylphs," the woman said, her white hair billowing behind her, making her look like a mirage against the bruised sky.

The men faded in and out of swirls, only for seconds at a time reforming into the thin, sharply featured bodies and faces they had been. I looked past them at the clouds, the tiny tornadoes breaking off—thousands of them—all heading away from me now.

"Where are they going?" I asked, my head still so heavy with fatigue.

A single flash of lightning blinded me for a second, except for the image of Djin's beautiful, exotic face, her black hair and thin, dark eyebrows pitching in excitement.

"They're going to war, water child!" She laughed, and the booming sound of it shattered the exhaustion weighing me down. It seemed to fall away like sheets of broken ice, leaving whole sections of my body lighter as fiery bolts again shot across the sky—another army charging in the same direction as the multitudes of tornadoes that spun across the wide, endless sky.

"Cora!" Reed echoed, the sound reaching through the air like a hawk's hunting cry, sharp and piercing until he pulled me under the skim. "What happened? Where did you go?" he demanded.

"They came," I echoed, the heaviness in my body gone except for the leaden grief I felt for Nicholas.

"Who?" He blew a rush of water through his gills, causing a million tiny bubbles to form behind him.

"*Them*." I smiled as the little bubbles combined into larger bubbles, then into two enormous bubbles like the one that carried me to the surface. They began pushing us in the direction of the lighting and the tornadoes.

"What is this?" Reed tried to dart away from his bubble, but it only found him again and pushed him on.

"Don't fight it. They're Sylphs," I explained." I told you. We're not alone."

"Where are they pushing us? *Cora!*"

I felt a heat spark, then spread in my chest. "To war."

Chapter 18

Reed and I followed the Sylph tornadoes toward Scrapper Island...toward The Shallows, our home. We were going to end this war before it spread any farther. End it before more people were killed.

I thought of Nicholas, how he stood against his own people to defend mine, even as many of them were attacking his ship. He could have assumed that Opal and I were like the Lawless, but he didn't. He didn't deserve to die, and I didn't think I would ever be able to forgive Reed for it.

Things would never be the same between us, and I had to accept that.

A bolt of lightning struck the water just ahead of me, throwing me off my trajectory. The green glow of St. Elmo's Fire hovered, undulating just above the skim until it took the form of a man. He stretched toward me, his long arms mock-swimming through the air. I started swimming away until he spoke.

"Hello, little sister." His thin lips pulled to a smile, and his voice was palpable—electric—on my skin. A crack of thunder filled the air as his eyebrows and hair took on the color of dark green, then deepened to black. The rain that was pelting my skin passed right through him while I watched his coloring shift like the Undines', but he encompassed the spectrum of yellows, blues, and greens, while we could only achieve the range of black to white.

Reed stopped in my wake, confused. "What's wrong?"

"You don't see...*him*?" It was the only way I could think to describe what I only assumed was one of Djin's Salamander Elementals.

"Who...?" Reed echoed warily, his airborne voice low and warning like a sea lion's bellow.

The Salamander flickered to bright green as he briefly bared his teeth at Reed." I should make a soup of him," he said, twirling his finger in a circle.

I swam in front of Reed. "No!" I echoed, holding up a hand.

The Salamander's wide smile wilted as he rolled his eyes. He dropped his spinning finger, and gave me an exhausted look. "Honestly, you really should make up your mind."

"What? I didn't ask you to do that!"

"Cora? What's happening?" Reed touched my shoulder, but I shrugged him off.

"Just stay quiet." I glared at him, still angry.

The Salamander laughed. "You didn't *have* to ask. I should boil him just for what he tried to do to that son of Eve."

"What he *tried* to do?" I waited for the answer without even allowing myself to blink. The Salamander's slow smile returned just long enough for me to see it before he dissipated into green and yellow wisps, then vanished in the rain. "Come back!" I echoed after him, but he was gone.

"*What's* going on?" Reed surfaced in front of me abruptly, but I didn't answer him before I dove into the water, renewed. "Cora!" The echo muffled from above the skim.

Could Nicholas have survived? I saw his blood. He was unconscious, unable to help himself even if he could have been saved. And if he wasn't dead, how was it that Reed and I were made Undine again after swallowing whatever that liquid was?

I swam faster than I ever had, onward to Scrapper Island. Onward to where Mama Luz's barge was waiting for Mara to return with the Guard, no doubt so they could become the leaders of her new, Lawless army.

Would she give them legs and send them onto land to invade, along with her feral creations? Would they also be utilized at sea? My mind was spinning with what she might be planning…with how I could outmaneuver her.

"*Cora!*" Reed's echoes continued to wash over me in the current, but I still couldn't divert my attention to answer them.

I swam even harder, running every possible scenario I could imagine through my mind. Even if I could regain control of the Guard, we would still be outnumbered by the Lawless. I needed to unite the Undine again. I needed to show them that Mama Luz was just using them all.

We finally reached the sandbar, but I didn't see Mama Luz's ship. Reed surfaced next to me, his chest heaving and his gills flaring.

"Where's the ship?" I echoed, scanning the outskirts of The Shallows surrounding the prison island. "Mara will be bringing the Guard there."

"*What*…is happening, Cora?" Reed demanded.

The rain fell harder and the wind picked up, causing the tide to heave. Webs of lightning reached across the sky again, some even striking the island.

"They're really here. Djin and Paralda really did send them…" I echoed.

Reed squared my shoulders and met my eyes. "Cora! Sent *who*? Tell me what's going on!"

"The other Elemental queens…they promised they would send help to sink Mama Luz's boat—I need to find the Lawless."

I dove under the surf and echoed a rally call for the Queen's Guard, though I didn't see any of them. I didn't pick up a response, either.

At least not from them.

The Shallows were filling with swells, clouding the water, but in the distance I saw a pod of Lawless Undine approaching…maybe five or six tritons and three or four sirens. They shimmered silver in the flashes of lightning that cut through the skim, and the reverberating thunder that sank through the water only served as a dramatic backdrop for their answering echoes.

"Well, hello, little pearl," one of the sirens cooed, her silver hair nearly glowing in the surreal green light that permeated the water around us. "We thought you ran away to the Southern Depths with your mommy."

"Listen to me." I tried to explain, but none of their venomous expressions changed. "I know Mama Luz promised you the world would be ours again, but it's because of her that we were banished to the water in the first place." They drew closer, encircling me. "Are you listening to what I'm saying? She was there in the days of Eden. So was my mother. Luz told her the humans wanted to make us their slaves so the Undines would help her rebel, but that was never true—listen to me!" I echoed again when none of the Lawless seemed to acknowledge anything I was explaining.

They dove at me, slicing at me with their fins. I reached for my short spear, forgetting that I didn't have it anymore. I didn't have any weapons at all except for my training.

"Where's your mommy, *Your Highness*?" one of the tritons echoed. His pale, silver face and chest were scarred with long, ragged marks from what must have been territory clashes. His armored scales were torn away in places, his fins ripped and split. I scanned the others and noticed they were all battle scarred in similar ways.

"*Please*, listen to me. We need to come together. Let me help you—don't you see that Luz is only using you?"

"Help *us*!?" one of them echoed while the rest laughed, the sound again rivaling the rolling thunder that shook the swells around us. I tried to dart upward, out of their closing circle, but there were too many of them.

"Move back!" Reed commanded as he darted toward the pod. He jutted his short spear at them, and my stomach lurched, remembering the sight of Nicholas's blood on it.

The pod just laughed again as four of the tritons broke off and surrounded him. The others closed the circle around me again and began slashing and jabbing the edges of their tails at me. One of the sirens jolted forward, but I moved aside and slapped her back with my tail, knocking her into the remaining triton. The two other sirens came from behind and bound my arms with my hair. Mara must have taught them because only members of the Guard knew how to tie those knots so quickly.

"Will you just *listen*? Mama Luz is immortal! She's responsible for us being banished from The Garden!"

"Come and tell her yourself," one of the sirens echoed. I somersaulted, whipping both of the ones behind me with my tail. They fell away long enough for me to cut my sloppy binds with my fin, but the remaining triton grabbed Reed's short spear as the others restrained him.

He held it to Reed's gills. "Are you done, *Princess*?" he echoed, the long scar down the side of his face wrinkling his mottled skin when he sneered at me. The tritons behind Reed bent his arms behind his back so tightly that his shoulders were pushed grotesquely forward, and I worried that they would be knocked out of joint.

"All right…" I echoed, holding up my palms.

One of the sirens hit me in the stomach with her tail, knocking me in the direction of The Shallows. "Go then!" The pod rippled with laughter again as we started to move.

I had to trust that Djin and Paralda would help us once we got to Mama Luz, though I wasn't sure how her ship could be overturned now without Nicholas.

My mind wandered back to him as we were driven through the water, and I let myself live in the possibility that he really could still be alive. The Salamander said that Reed *tried* to kill Nicholas, I repeated to myself… When I pressed him on it, he just grinned and drifted away. Nothing about that reaction would make any sense unless he knew something I didn't.

Why wouldn't the Salamander have just told me? Why the games?

Djin and Parada had also played games. I started to get angry. Maybe that's how their kind were because they had the luxury of *options* all these centuries—to come and go over the earth as they pleased while the Undines were banished to the water.

I wasn't made for games. I had to decide on an action because bouncing among so many unknowns would make me lose my mind. I had to believe.

Somewhere, Nicholas *was* still alive.

Chapter 19

The pod of Lawless brought Reed and me to the largest school of Undines I'd ever seen. They had overrun the boundary lines of The Shallows and taken over, but there was no sign of Mara or the Guard. No sign of my mother, Enoch, or Shoal.

And no sign of Nicholas or his ship on the heaving, tossing skim. *He's alive... He has to be alive...* I repeated to myself.

Mama Luz's boat was anchored in the same place I'd left it along the sandbar. The undulating tide pitched it out of the water in places, crashing it back down again and submerging nearly half of the hull. It had to be midday by now, but the world above was dark with storm clouds, the only exceptions being the explosions of lightning exchanges that continuously raked the sky.

There wasn't a length of water in any direction that wasn't occupied by countless Lawless, every one of them, as far as I could tell, scarred from decades of fighting, brutal, and angry.

I had no idea what would happen next. There were too many possibilities, too many variables, too much I didn't know.

And I was *supposed* to know.

Hundreds of Lawless rode the undertows with no regard for the danger they were in when they shot over the arcing waves into the open air, then dove back into the water.

"Don't you see the storm?" I echoed to those who were closest. "You can't breach when it's like this!" I tried to warn, but none of them listened. The Lawless were from The Depths—their gills larger to offset the pressure they'd adapted to, their eyes smaller—and the only time they ever surfaced was when they were attacking ships. The only thing greater than their naivety at this point was their stupid pride.

I'd barely finished this thought when a blinding flash of lightning ripped through the sky. It lingered in a pulsing explosion for several seconds while the deafening crack of thunder seemed to shake the earth itself, the tremors driving straight through the twenty or so feet of water this close to the island.

When the tremors passed, large pieces of debris rained into the skim. I thought it might have been pieces of Mama Luz's boat or maybe coconuts pulled from their trees by the wind, but as the pieces sunk, I realized they were neither of these things. They were the remains of those Lawless Undines who rode the undertows and breached themselves into the air just now, despite my warning.

I squeezed my eyes shut when a Lawless siren's scarred arm washed in front of me, pushed and pulled by the violent, crashing waves. But even with my eyes closed, I couldn't erase the image…the blackened skin and flayed scales, the muscles severed by what looked like claw marks clear down to the bones.

If I had any doubt the Sylphs and Salamanders were indeed here, it was erased. This was not natural lightning —it was something more. But they were killing my people, and this was never what I wanted.

I never would have agreed to their help if I knew they were going to kill the Lawless, but I couldn't find words to form, to shape into an echo that would be enough to stop the horror playing out around me.

The sound I made instead was grief. Grief for Nicholas and for the hundreds of Lawless who were destroyed just seconds ago.

It was the sound of decades of fear and anger and resentment, but most of all, it was the unequivocal, absolute call for everything—for every single thing including the raging, unbridled sea—to stop and listen.

To my amazement, the lightning and wind did stop as the water churned in the aftermath. The driving rain was replaced by softer, sparser drops until they, too, stopped falling.

The Lawless had all turned to me as far as I could see in the tossed waters. I knew there were thousands of them in any direction, and again I called so loudly that I was sure I would be heard at the top and bottom of the world, under glaciers, and in the boiling pools that lay at the center of the Earth.

"I have something to confess to you," I echoed, marveling at how clear it all suddenly was. "I have been your leader, but I have not led, and you were right not to follow me. I wouldn't have followed a coward either."

"*Cora...*" Reed echoed softly from somewhere behind me, but I wouldn't be silenced now.

I smiled at him. "You have always protected me. But I should have been the one protecting you." I nodded and turned back to the Lawless, who looked both shocked and confused as the waters began to clear. "Over the past three days I've learned that we have been manipulated for centuries into believing that humans were our enemies, but our real enemy was The Gnome Queen *Ghob*," I explained, feeling the reverberations in the water starting again. "Her name is not *Mama Luz*, and she cannot *give us* the world back. I've learned what she knew all along. If we follow her, we'll only be helping her take it for herself."

The Lawless began to jeer and protest, some of them even began advancing on me.

"Did your *mommy* tell you this, Princess?" a large triton echoed, and though I couldn't see him in the disturbed water, I felt him advancing. Several others echoed in agreement, the sound revealing their ranks closing around him as a wall of them began moving toward me.

"No, my mother did not tell me. I only wish she had," I answered without moving. "It was the Elemental Queen of the Air, Paralda, and Djin, the Elemental Queen of the Great Fire." I felt the wall of Lawless stop abruptly, so I advanced on them. "And when I find my mother, my first question will be the one you have right now as well. *Why were we not told of the others like us in the world?*"

"I had no choice," my mother echoed from somewhere beyond the murky water. Some of the Lawless closest to me bared their teeth at the sound of her voice, and for an instant, I thought they might all charge in her direction. But another small echo broke through before they could mobilize.

"Cora...*Cora*!" Opal darted out of the opaque waters toward me. Her little arms were welted, and there were ragged gashes over her shoulder.

"Opal! What happened to you?" I echoed, squaring her shoulders in front of me so I could scan her.

"I couldn't catch up with the Guard to the Southern Depths, so I just swam there on my own," she said with not a little pride." I made it, Cora. I told them about Mama Luz and..." She trailed off when she saw Reed over my shoulder, her shock vanishing almost as quickly as it appeared. She rocketed toward him, throwing her arms around his waist. The tritons holding Reed backed away at the sight of Enoch and Shoal, each of them equal in strength to fifty Lawless.

My mother smiled, her long, narrow face looking paler than normal as she lowered her large, yellow eyes. "I owe you an explanation," she echoed, and after a few more seconds, lifted her head to the Lawless. "I owe all of you an explanation!"

She went on to explain about The Garden of Eden, how we were all once welcome there until Ghob had lied to her, and the Undines had been banished from The Garden as a result.

Some of the Lawless clamored near the surface and surrounded Mama Luz's ship as my mother explained how the Gnome War started. That *she* started it as futile revenge, and that the treaty we shared now was nothing more than a guarantee that if we stopped attacking her ships, Ghob would watch over the Undines who had been stranded on land. Those who would always be called to the sea, but could never return. My father was one of these Undine.

My mother turned to me. "Surely by now he is no longer alive, but his lineage, that of the others…they all must be protected." She shook her head, her wide eyes pleading. "I didn't tell you about his fate because I didn't want you to have a lifetime consumed by war and revenge…like mine."

I didn't have time to process any of this before Mara began barking her protest. "So in protecting your princess, you abandoned the Lawless. For *centuries*," she echoed from somewhere far below us, but rising. I felt the push of the Queen's Guard behind her in the refracting sound.

"Do you think you're their savior?" I called into the deep green water. "Tell us, Mara. Is Dynah with you? Dynah of The Depths!" I echoed for her, knowing I would not get a reply. "You sliced her throat. You were ready to betray all the Lawless for your own gain, just like Mama Luz did to my mother all those years ago." I turned toward the horizon, toward the Lawless I couldn't see, but knew had gathered. "Don't you see? Mara would happily exchange all of you for a chance to return to land!"

"Desperate cries from a desperate, weak princess," Mara echoed. I felt her advancing again. The Guard moved with her, so I turned to face them.

"She betrayed Reed of The Shallows, one of our own lieutenants, to Mama Luz. She left him with her to die. Did she tell you that? When I came for him, she had promised Luz *your* loyalty in exchange for my capture.

Ask yourselves… Are you willing to serve the Gnome Queen? To be slaves to a selfishness that has already cost too many lives?" I darted into the murky water, to Mara, stopping when we were eye to eye. "You will *not* enslave my people."

"You had your chance to lead, *Princess*," Mara echoed, gripping her short spear. "Now, you can die."

She jabbed her spear into my rib, in between the armored scales as we'd been trained by Shoal and Enoch. I darted to the side, but not before I felt the searing pain of the sharpened edge slice my skin. The wide planes of Mara's face shifted from silver to black with the sudden violence, only returning to silver when she pulled the spear back.

"Cora!" Reed echoed. The rows of Mara's small, needle-like teeth slowly faded into the dark waters as I drifted backward, still unsure of what just happened, or how bad the damage was. My mind was racing, but it felt as if everything were retreating at the same time. Clouding. Vanishing.

Flashes of light electrified the sky again, followed by bellows of thunder that moved through my whole body. I drifted in the water, aware of movement all around me, but detached from it, like I was somehow invisible and powerless to affect it. It was so tempting to close my eyes and let it all slip away. To stop fighting a war that could never be won because my greatest enemy was never who I thought. It was never the Lawless or Mara or even Mama Luz.

What became the solitary thought in my mind was that my greatest enemy all these years—the one who had played the role of leader but never took the necessary risks...*not really*—had been me.

<h1 style="text-align:center">Chapter 20</h1>

I heard my mother's location echo calling desperately to me. It bounced off the waves until it found me, but I knew she wouldn't be able to follow it because she was cut off by the streams of mobilizing Lawless. Reed's echo sounded next, but he, too, was cut off. Mara must have delivered the Guard to Mama Luz, and soon they would lead the Lawless toward land. *Toward the humans.*

I thought of the stories Nicholas told me of his people. Of Bev and those who lived in The Grind lands, forgotten, feared, and at best, tolerated beyond the gates of The Citadel...just like our Lawless. I closed my eyes under the weight of the thought. *How had we lived all these centuries worlds apart, yet made so many of the same mistakes?*

The pain in my side spread, and my clouded senses made my head feel heavy, like I was sinking farther and farther down. I heard Reed's location echo again, still cut off by the streams of Lawless who were creating countercurrents to the tide pummeling the shore.

I had to stop them. There had to be a way. I forced myself to swim upward, to sound my trajectory, to echo loudly enough to rival the thunder when I broke through the skim. The pain from Mara's spear was almost unbearable, and Mama Luz's ship was advancing over the tossing sea. The Lawless were following her into the second wave of the storm, which was black and rolling on the horizon.

"Stop!" I echoed, my airborne voice barely audible in the thunder that continually shook the sky. If Paralda and

Djin had been helping me—and they had to have been, or I wouldn't have survived Mara's spear—they seemed to have forgotten me now.

But I couldn't go back to my protected world anymore and do nothing. I may have failed my own people by hiding behind boundary walls my entire life, but I would die before I failed Nicholas's too. It was what he would do. It was what leaders do.

I swam until the ache in my side forced me to slow, but I didn't stop. If I had to arrive at the front lines of the Lawless with a school of sharks in my wake, that's what I would do, as long as it meant stopping Mama Luz.

The tide was strong, and I didn't know how much longer I would be able to swim against it below the skim. I would never catch the front lines of the Lawless at this rate, so I pressed my arm into my side and began to cut the water like the dolphins, using the undertow of the pending waves to pull forward, breach, and dive again into the pull of the water. I could only hope Djin would be watching and would keep her Salamanders from electrocuting me in mid-breach like the hundreds of Lawless who had met this fate before me.

The cold rain pelted my back and tail as the clouds rolled, gathering and growling like something alive and hunting. I thought of Paralda and how very real that idea could be, which was comforting until I saw that even the massive gales she must have been creating were not enough to stop Mama Luz's ship or the army of Lawless Undine following her toward the horizon.

But the wind had blown something else into view.

An enormous ship emerged from the storm, at least four times the size of Mama Luz's barge. As the ship moved closer, I closed the rest of the distance even though it felt like one more jump would tear me in half. I had to get in front of the Lawless.

Mama Luz's barge started to arc out of the way, but the white ship began firing on it anyway—firing on the *Lawless* in the water.

"No!" I echoed, launching toward it with the intent to sink it myself if it fired on the Undines again. I rammed the side of the hull, barely cracking it. Intense pain shot through my side, and I channeled the imminent cry into a command. "Stop! Or I will drag you to the bottom of the sea myself!" I wailed into the howling wind.

"Cora…?" Nicholas called down to me over the railing. I could barely hear him, barely see him, and wasn't sure it really *was* him until I saw several deckhands rush to the railing and pull him back from it.

He was alive… I didn't know how, but he *was* alive.

A rolling laughter, thick and heavy, filled the air. The wind lessened and the lighting fell into rivulets of St. Elmo's Fire, which took the shape of countless Salamander Elementals lighting the sky. Tornado whips pulled from the clouds and shifted into the forms of long, wispy Sylphs. More Lawless surfaced from under the skim, and all eyes were on me.

"Well, it been a busy tree days fer ya, little princess…" Mama Luz's voice surrounded me. "But I smell yer blood on de water."

"I know all your lies, *Ghob*!" I echoed over the heads of the countless Lawless gathered in the water. "I know how you let the Undine *die* just so you could have the world for yourself!"

Mama Luz laughed again. "De only ones who died was da ones already dead, my fishy!" she said, but I still couldn't see her on her ship. "To and from da water of life dey went, toting it on der backs like slaves to dem new pets in da Garden dat *I made*. Eatin' up all de fruits dat *I made*. We was gods, little princess! Da Mother made us gods, not slaves!"

A lifeboat started lowering down the side of Nicholas's ship, and I glanced to find him fighting with two of the other men aboard. He pushed one away and hit the other one who was advancing on him again.

"Cora! Hold on!" he shouted as he jumped over the railing and landed hard in the boat. I started getting dizzy in the heave of the tide pushing me up, then disappearing and leaving me to crash back into the water.

"What was wrong with helping them?" I echoed, the pain in my side sharpening again where Mara had tried to stab me. I gripped a piece of the cracked hull for support and pressed my arm into the wound again. "We were supposed *to teach* them!"

Mama Luz finally appeared on her deck, her dark braids blowing in every direction underneath her red scarf, which also whipped behind her in the breeze. She reached out to the sea with her strong, bared arms, the flowing green sleeves turning black with rain against her dark skin.

She laughed obnoxiously this time and let her head fall back. "Help dem…*teach* dem…" she mocked. "Yer not listenin', water child!" She raised one arm to the sky. "Do ya tink deez sprites had da same burden as yer kind and mine? Deez smug little fairies flittin' in de skies? Dey never seen Da Fadder's pets destroy what *dey* made from der little cloud perches."

"We let you back in The Garden, *Ghob*, or have you forgotten?" Djin said, her voice coming from a growing lightning storm low in the sky. "You retrieved the seeds to begin again." She emerged from storm, draped in the shifting colors of St. Elmo's Fire, just like the Salamander who came to me before.

"Outta guilt you let me in! Guilt because ya knew my burden. It was de *least* to be done," Mama Luz answered spitefully.

"And what of Necksa's burden?" Paralda asked, moving toward us all from the center of three merging tornadoes. She held her long, thin face tightly as her white hair flared and faded into the clouds behind her. "You are not the tortured one here, Ghob."

"Cora…Cora, can you hear me?" Nicholas said, the lifeboat just out of reach. Lawless snapped at the oars as he rowed as far as the rope still attached to the deck would allow. It was enough. I gripped the side of the boat, and he pulled me aboard. "Christ, Cora…" He pressed a cloth against my side and stared at me, somehow knowing the questions I couldn't ask. "They came…the fire ones," he said, showing me the ragged burn mark on his throat." Then the wind ones came and brought me to land—to this ship, and back here…to you."

It wasn't more than a second later that the boat was rocked so hard I was thrown free, back into the water.

"It's all right, Cora," my mother echoed, the feeling of her voice warm and heavy all around me. Everything else stilled, even the waves. She pressed her hand to my side and light cleared the murky waters, revealing the leagues of stunned Lawless and schools of whales far in the distance.

My body went numb, but then felt warm again. Stronger.

I shot up through the skim, high above Mama Luz's ship, and grabbed her arms on the way down. Her clay minions followed her as I pulled her into the sea, each of them crashing into the water around us. By the time their impact bubbles cleared, they were already dissolving, and soon, there was nothing left of them. I turned again to Mama Luz, her wide, electric grin beaming in the water before me. She laughed open-mouthed as bubbles escaped. I thought I would drown her, that it would be over, but my grip on her arms seemed to loosen as my fingers sank into her flesh.

Her long, dark braids turned to sand and washed away, followed by her ears, her shoulders, every piece of her dissolving to earth and leaving only her gaping, laughing mouth, which also finally disappeared along with the sound of her all-encompassing laughter.

"Coward!" I echoed, the sound ripping a hole in the length of Mama Luz's barge and ricocheting off anything else in its path. The Lawless surrounding me parted, and I heard Nicholas in the distance. He was about to impale one of the Lawless with his oar as he straddled the capsized lifeboat.

"Nicholas! Stop!" I echoed, knowing he wouldn't understand, but I hoped the screeching bird call would be enough to get his attention.

He looked up, and the Lawless he was about to kill knocked him into the water. I darted to him and righted the boat, commanding the siren he almost killed to back away from him.

She obeyed. In fact, all the Lawless backed away. The gnashing water evened and the dark, electric clouds rolled back behind the horizon.

"Cora!" Reed echoed. In his wake, Shoal and Enoch carried my mother to me. I left Nicholas once he'd climbed back into the boat and swam back to my mother.

"What's wrong? What happened to her?" I demanded. Her yellow, glowing eyes were dim, and her silver skin was dull and tacky with the same kind of white film Reed had aboard Mama Luz's boat.

"She is passing, water child." Paralda's voice surrounded me. My mother's hair dried in the warm breeze and draped over her long body. "She gave her immortality to heal you."

"No! No...take it back! Give it back to her!" I demanded of the shimmering green and yellow light that surrounded her. "*Djin*! You healed Nicholas! Give it back to her!"

"Cora..." my mother said, reaching for me. I took her hand and held it to my chest.

"You're going to be all right, Mother. Djin can heal you."

"No, my dear…"

"Yes! She brought Nicholas back! I watched him die, but she brought him back. She can help!"

My mother just smiled at me. "The only person who could heal me is you, Cora. And you've already done that."

"No, I haven't done anything. This is all happening because of me!"

"Yes…" My mother tried to laugh. "You've brought my sisters back to me. You've ended centuries of hatred and blame, Cora. And you have united our people," she said, raising her eyes to the sea of Undine, Lawless and Royal Guard shoulder to shoulder. "You are their queen now. Their warrior queen. Lead them and protect them."

"Mother… I'm not ready. Mother, no. No! *Please*…" I echoed.

"Believe, my child. Believe in yourself as I do. This is not the end… it is only a new beginning…"

The water lapped over her arms, which became white with foam. Slowly, she washed away from me, illuminated on the tide that had shifted direction in the breeze, the glow of St. Elmo's Fire surrounding her until she disappeared in all directions of the vast, endless sea.

Epilogue

We would not be able to return to The Shallows. There were too many of us now that the Undines were united. Mara had escaped any justice that could befall her, but that didn't matter anymore. The Lawless had exiled her, which meant she would be killed on sight if she dared show her face again.

I wondered if she'd gone in search of Mama Luz, who was likely putting herself back together one grain of sand at a time. I didn't know how long it would take before she surfaced again. I only knew she would, and it was my duty until the end of eternity to protect my people from her.

"Captain, the squadron is en route to escort the human—er, *Nicholas's* ship to the island, as you ordered, The rest of us should catch up with them by tomorrow," one of the Guard lieutenants echoed to Reed. He nodded in acknowledgment before pulling away from Opal, leaving her with her parents as he swam to my side.

"I... I would apologize to him for what I did if he could understand me," Reed echoed quietly after a long pause.

"I know you would. But we're all on the same side now." I smiled at him. "It's in the past."

"It's not, though, as much as I wish I could just leave it there." He checked our distance from the Guard over his shoulder and turned back to me. "You should know, too, I would do it again, Cora...if the price of your life was his. I would do it again, even though he's a good person." I looked into his eyes, narrowed in sincerity as his silver brows drew together and his jaw tightened." Even if the price of your life was *mine*."

I opened my mouth to respond, but he nodded to me and swam ahead before I could even have the chance. I darted after him.

"Reed!" I echoed, hooking his arm. The way he looked at me was different, though. Distant. He was Captain of my Guard again, and I was his queen.

"Luz can track you now because of that *thing* that bit you by the island Shallows. She has an advantage," he warned, completely changing the subject. He didn't meet my eyes, and I knew I would have to be content to let his distance go. For now.

"Dr. Zee called what bit me a *Feral*," I echoed, glancing at the outline of the scar left by the bite. I had to hope that once Nicholas led us back to Snake Island, Dr. Zee would know how to neutralize whatever made me trackable—that he would know what to do about the monsters Mama Luz had already set loose in the world. And maybe, that he would even be able to help me walk on land again, if only for a little while.

But there were no guarantees, and I wasn't yet sure how we would help Nicholas fight this war. I only knew that we would.

"Cora?" Reed echoed impatiently. "Did you hear me? Who's Dr. Zee?" Several seconds passed before I found my way back into the moment, and I slowly realized I hadn't told him the whole story of what happened on the island we were returning to now. I turned to Reed, and this time, albeit briefly, he met my eyes. "I mean, if you want to tell me…"

So much had happened since I'd left The Shallows the first time in pursuit of Reed, and I wasn't sure what would happen once we made our way back to Snake Island with Nicholas. I didn't know what the future held for humanity or for The Undines, but I was confident I could tell the story of how we had come to be united here now, once again.

"Of course, I'll tell you." I smiled as we picked up speed. "In the beginning…"

Nervous Water is the first book in the YA Fantasy series, *Elemental Wars*, a spinoff from the Dystopian Sci-Fi/ Supernatural Thriller series, *First Bloods*, noted below.

***

If you liked *Nervous Water*, please consider leaving a review at mybook.to/NERVOUSWATER. These go a long way to helping authors like me find cool readers like you.

First Bloods Companion Series:

ELEMENTAL WARS
- ◆ Book 1: *Nervous Water*

EDEN'S BLUFF ACADEMY
- ◆ Book 1: *Poisoned Garden* (2020)

~~~~~~

Want to grab a free copy of *Feral*, the prequel to the *First Bloods* series? Join my VIP Reader Group at
bit.ly/TracyKornNL

FIRST BLOODS
- ◆ Prequel: *Feral*
- ◆ Book 1: *Bad Seed*
- ◆ Book 2: *Bitter Fruit* (2020)
- ◆ Book 3: *Killing Frost* (2020)
~~~~~~

About Tracy Korn

Tracy Korn is a sci-fi / fantasy author and all around science geek who may or may not have a"Lip Smackers" chapstick addiction.

When she's not inventing dystopian worlds (and subsequently saving them or wrecking them more), she reads about other people doing it, practices her newbie cinematographer skills, and dreams of someday meeting James Cameron.

*To be the first to hear about new releases, giveaways, and if Tracy ever really does meet James Cameron, sign up for her VIP Reader Group at **bit.ly/TracyKornNL***

Don't forget to stop by social media for impromptu giveaways, or just to hang out!

- www.facebook.com/AuthorTracyKorn
- twitter.com/Tracybonics
- instagram.com/tracy_korn
- bit.ly/TracyKornGoodreads
- bit.ly/TracyKornBookBub